CW00860241

The Price of FREEDOM IN *1848*

JOHN SWISHER

outskirts press

The Price of Freedom in 1848

v3.0

This is a work of fiction. Names, characters, businesses, places, events, locales, and incidents are either the products of the author's imagination or used in a fictitious manner. Any resemblance to actual persons, living or dead, or actual events is purely coincidental.

The opinions expressed in this manuscript are solely the opinions of the author and do not represent the opinions or thoughts of the publisher. The author has represented and warranted full ownership and/or legal right to publish all the materials in this book.

Outskirts Press, Inc.
http://www.outskirtspress.com

Paperback ISBN: 978-1-9772-2718-8
Hardback ISBN: 978-1-9772-2722-5

PRINTED IN THE UNITED STATES OF AMERICA

Dedication to Kimeta Warwick Dover
An inspiration for us all.

Acknowledgments

Many people have helped with this book. Judy, my wife, had read and edited drafts of chapters before they were submitted. She kept me off the web and on Word to get this story out. She also helped with basic research in the Library of Virginia in Richmond and went with me to meetings with Kimeta Warwick Dover. Judy saw the Limoges porcelain in Kimeta's cabinet that is mentioned in this book. She has been a dedicated and loving partner in this effort.

Vicki Entreken has been an outstanding coach and editor. She helped me focus on the purpose of this book and with better development of scenes and characters. Vicki also helped make the dialogue more realistic. She identified major events that were missing from an earlier version, e.g., life on the Warwick plantation and Martha's marriage. I will always be grateful for her work on my behalf.

My family in Madison Heights deserves a special thanks. They first told me about this story and Kimeta's visit to find a slave graveyard. They sat through readings of chapters and encouraged me along the way. They also shared the oral history of their farmhouse apparently built on the foundation of the Warwick plantation home. We went on tours of Lynchburg, Virginia, to visit the

Friends meetinghouse, Jubal Early's redoubt, and numerous other sites.

A special thanks to many friends who have checked on my progress and encouraged me to keep working.

Part I

Life on a Quaker Plantation
Whose unmarked grave?

The Slave Act was written to encourage other white free people to hunt down and capture escaped slaves.

Virginia Law (1705)

Summer, 1847, Spring Hill Plantation outside Lynchburg, Virginia

Chapter 1
Patrollers Can Be Rude

Martha sprawled out on the roof of the kitchen house, looked up into the dark sky, and quietly named the constellations. She pulled a folded piece of paper from under a roof shingle and checked to see if she was right. Master Warwick had shown her a book with drawings of the stars, and he let her copy the page. Her favorite was the Big Dipper. It was easy to see, and it looked just like the ladle she used to serve soup. Master Warwick said that the Big Dipper pointed to the North Star and that it rotated around the bright star as the seasons changed, but it always pointed north. The free states were in the north. Instead of the North Star, she liked to call it the freedom star. She would follow it one day to freedom. One day soon.

Slave catchers galloped on the long lane toward Spring Hill Plantation. Hound dogs kept pace, whining for action. Al, who was the stockier of the two men, looked down at his Cuban bloodhound and said, "Don't you worry now. We gonna catch us a runner before the night's over." The two jumped down and stomped onto the pillared porch of a Quaker's plantation home. The building was two stories but did not have an elaborate staircase to the porch. The tall windows were bordered with simple shutters. Al pounded on the door. Martha stayed hidden.

Frederick Jr., who was a house servant wearing the proper attire of pants, white shirt, and vest, glanced through the curtains covering a narrow glass window and frowned. Opening the door about a foot, he said, "How can I help you?"

"You hidin' a runner?" asked a well-dressed man sporting a bow tie.

"No sir," said Frederick Jr., a little concerned that these slave catchers would disturb his master.

"I want to talk to John Warwick."

"He is not well and has retired for the night."

This pair had been here before with accusations that this plantation was a stop on the Underground Railroad. They were officially known as "patrollers," and the slaves called them "pattyrollers." Their dogs lost the scent in the woods near the main road close to the lane leading here.

"Well, he won't mind then if we take a look around," the man said, and then they headed toward the slave cabins.

Spring Hill Plantation had a dozen slave cabins lined up in two rows, built close together. They each had two rooms, including one bedroom and a loft where the younger children slept. Any more than that, and they slept on the floor. John Warwick assigned Frederick Jr.'s family to the nearest cabin. They all worked in the big house when guests were entertained, which was often. Nails in the log walls served as a place to hang the few clothes they possessed. Special care was given to their big house servant clothes. A pot hung over the smoldering fire, and the cabin smelled of vegetable stew.

Frederick was working on a sermon, leafing through a Bible and copying phrases from his American Bible Society version. His standard sermon message was, if they believed in Jesus, they would be free in heaven. His wife, Lucy, was at the table nursing their one-year-old son, and three kids were asleep in the loft.

The ruckus at the big house interrupted his preparation. Men were now banging on the doors of the nearby cabins. Frederick quickly hid his Bible behind the fireplace logs and turned as Wesley, his fifteen-year-old son, was climbing down from the loft. "Wes, go out the back door and get the lantern off the barn as fast as you can."

Bowtie and Al barged into the cabin. Bowtie was wearing a gun visible with his navy-blue wool coat open. Al was unshaven and wore an old, ragged shirt and matching pants. Ankle cuffs hung from his belt, and he carried a whip. He grabbed the remains of a loaf of bread from the table and shoved half of it into his grey-toothed mouth.

Pointing to the loft, Al asked with his mouth full, "Who you got up there?"

"My girls," Frederick said. Al moved toward the ladder, and Frederick stepped in his way. "They is sleeping." Al pushed him to the floor and climbed the squeaking ladder. Bowtie laughed and said, "Have a look, Al."

Al held his lantern up. He smelled like he hadn't washed for a week.

"Just one little darkie up here," he said and climbed back down.

Lucy and Frederick shared a concerned look with only one asleep in the loft. Lucy, trembling, stood up and covered the baby with a rag. Al glared at her and shoved another chunk of bread in his mouth. He lurched toward her, causing her to step back and fall onto the bench. The rag fell to the dirt floor, and the baby started to cry. Frederick moved to get up, and Bowtie pulled out his pistol. Lucy covered the baby and moved him back to her breast to stop him from crying, but Al was now in her face. He pulled the rag away, looked at the baby, and grinned, his grey teeth still working the bread. He looked up at Lucy, and she froze, his foul breath on her chest. Then, with one finger, he reached down and pushed the baby off her nipple. The little one screamed, and the man grinned at Lucy. Then he turned to Frederick and laughed.

"Check that out," Bowtie said, pointing to the back room.

Al went in, looked around, and then banged out the small back door. He whistled to his hounds, who eagerly joined him. He pounded on the side of the cabin as they sniffed around the area. They had the scent from a piece of clothing. Coming back around to the front, he leaned into the doorway and said, "Our man ain't here."

Suddenly, Jack stepped in front of Al and ducked as he came inside the cabin, still wearing his soiled work clothes. He saw Frederick on the floor, and Lucy and the baby were crying. "What's going on? Put that pistol away."

"Who are you?" said Bowtie.

Putting a hand on the pistol in his own belt, Jack said, "I'm the overseer here."

Bowtie put his pistol in his holster and folded the flap. Frederick took a deep breath and stood up.

"Now, why don't you get out of here," Jack said, "and let my people rest."

Wesley came in the front door, swinging a lantern.

"Where you bin?" asked Al.

"Checking on chicks," Wesley responded as Frederick took the lantern and set it by the fireplace.

"We want to search that barn," said Bowtie, backing away from Jack.

Jack hesitated and looked at both slave catchers. "Suit yourselves, but be quick about it. Keep them dogs quiet and away from the animals."

Martha had been watching from the roof. She didn't realize she had been holding her breath. Seeing the pattyrollers head to the barn, she gasped. She ran to her cabin and started up the ladder. Frederick said, "You'll get in trouble some night."

"I'm sorry, Daddy," she said and climbed the ladder. Once on her mattress, she had trouble going to sleep. Wesley crawled onto the straw mattress next to the wall. It wasn't long before he was snoring. Her sister, Prissy, had not stirred.

Patrollers were a continuous threat to any slave. Plantation owners hired them to return their "property" in working order. But they didn't care if runners were roughed up a bit in the process. Besides that, a colored man walking in broad daylight without papers could be cuffed, taken to the auction, and sold.

Martha heard the front door squeak and large boots scuffling. Then loud chewing downstairs. Was Frederick Jr. back from the big house? His duty usually lasted all night. She was afraid to look through her knothole. Suddenly, the ladder squeaked. Light reflected off the low ceiling. She could smell him. He raised his whip and lashed it. The thong and popper seemed to hang in the air above her head until she bolted upright and scraped her head on a beam. She grabbed her head, and her eyes darted around the loft. She didn't realize she had been dreaming. Wes and Prissy slept, but Al wasn't there. He wasn't anywhere in the cabin.

She sat on the straw mattress, took a deep breath, and rubbed her eyes. There would be no more sleeping that night. With her sandals tucked under an arm of her tattered knee-length work shirt, she snuck down the ladder, keeping her feet near the sides of the rungs so the ladder wouldn't squeak. Slowly opening the door, she slipped outside.

As the sun cracked over the horizon behind her, Martha walked along the dirt lane between the cabins. Ahead, Patrick stepped out of his cabin with a lunch box under his arm. He took big strides down the lane toward the barn. He was ten years older than Martha, but that didn't calm her interest. Why was he up so early? She followed him, tiptoeing and ducking between the cabins. His tattered field shirt covered broad shoulders, and his elbows showed through worn holes.

Patrick took his lunch inside the barn. Master Warwick hobbled up with his cane and leaned against the side of the barn. What were all of these people doing up early? Martha ducked further behind a cabin to make sure she wasn't seen. A few minutes later, Patrick came out empty-handed.

"Thank you, Patrick," Master Warwick said. "I appreciate your help."

"Yes sir," said Patrick, and he nodded.

Inside the barn, the hay-covered floor rose. Two blinking eyes looked around, a man grabbed the box, and the floor closed again. Martha gasped. When she looked back at the men, they were watching her, whispering.

"Hello, Martha," said Master Warwick. "Come over here." She hesitated, then walked over. "How are your star studies going?" he asked. Master Warwick, who was a Quaker, was always friendly and treated all of his people with kindness.

"Good."

"That's fantastic. You keep it up," he said, patting her shoulder. Then he hobbled back toward the big house. When she turned back toward the barn, Patrick wasn't anywhere around.

Inside, the barn smelled of cow manure, and the goats made themselves known. The floor of the barn was supposed to be dirt, but not today. Now, she knew there were runaways hidden under the floor, waiting for the right chance to run north, and she wanted to go with them. Martha kicked some of the hay near the opening and pulled on a makeshift handle. A black man flat on his back and chewing on some bread whispered, "What you want?"

Martha studied the man, who was old, and he already had a black eye. How far had he already run to get here? Suddenly, Patrick appeared and grabbed her arm.

"She wants to mind her own business," he said, and then he squeezed. She pulled her arm loose and tried to kick him, but he pushed her away from the hatch, and she fell backward to the floor near one of the stacks of hay. Patrick carefully replaced the floor covering and knocked three times on the door. The old man answered with two.

Patrick glared at Martha. "Don't you dare tell anyone what you saw," he hissed. He bent down to her face. "If you do, you Patrick answer to me."

She realized how angry she'd made him, and her lip quivered. Patrick sighed and grabbed Martha by the arm to help her up. She straightened her shirtdress and brushed hay from her back. She sniffled when he leaned down to her ear and whispered, "Remember what I said."

Martha could smell coffee on his breath. Then he nudged her toward the barn door. "Get on with you now," he said.

The workers were gathering next to the barn. Some would follow Jack out to the tobacco fields. Bill assigned local chores and then took the other group to the cotton fields. If you were six, you were picking cotton. Martha sprinted to the pens, past the chickens, hogs, and dogs, and then back to the barn. Jack was straining his neck, looking over the group of people when Martha appeared next to him.

"There you are, Martha. What happened to you?" She faltered, trying to come up with an explanation. She looked over at Patrick, and he glared back. When she opened her mouth to speak, Jack said, "I mean, look at ya." He pulled a stick of hay from her hair and tossed it to the ground. "How many we got?"

Martha sighed in relief. "Twenty-eight chickens, thirteen hogs, sir."

"And . . .?"

"Eight pigs. Nine, including Patrick," she said firmly, her chin raised. Jack grinned at Patrick, and the group chuckled. One of the kids poked Patrick, and his glare turned into a threatening fist. Martha sighed in relief, and then she smiled back at Patrick.

"All right, then, let's get moving."

Martha walked alongside Annise as she pushed the wheelbarrow toward the cookhouse. The food scraps were waiting for them. Annise was pretty, but according to Martha, she was a slow reader. She lifted the bucket with strong arms, scooped up scraps of food left from a weekend of guests at the big house, and dumped it into the wheelbarrow, never concerned that the scraps smelled like rancid meat and eggs. The girls were used to it. Annise was fifteen already, and Martha looked up to her. She wanted to be like her, except for the slow reading part. She often imagined what a big sister would be like. The girls went next to the chickens and started sorting out buckets of greens and peelings.

"I saw Patrick this morning," Martha said.

"Did he speak to you?" Annise pulled a long potato peel from the pile and tossed it into her bucket while grabbing several with her other hand. The girl was fast.

"Oh yeah," Martha said.

Annise stopped and looked at her. Then she leaned toward Martha. "Well, what did he say?"

"Well," Martha hesitated, "he said he'd kill me if I told anyone."

"Well, now, I'm not just anyone. You know we shares our secrets," Annise said. She cocked her head.

"If you promise not to tell anyone, I'll tell you some of it."

"OK, I'll see if some's enough."

"Patrick's helping a runaway hide in the barn. When I found the hideout, he pushed me down."

Annise became silent. Then she went back to picking through the food. After a few moments, Martha wondered if she'd even heard her. Did she say too much? Martha picked up a handful of scraps, but she kept watching Annise, waiting. Maybe she already knew?

Annise stole a quick glance at Martha, then took a deep breath. "We ain't 'posed to talk about stuff like that," she said. Martha knew that much.

"Fine. I won't say no more then," Martha said.

"There's more?"

Martha hesitated and then said, "I almost climbed in there with him."

"Did not! You lie!" Annise threw a corncob at her, and it bounced off Martha's shoulder. The girls laughed. Then Martha went silent.

"One day," she mumbled. Annise saw the serious look on Martha's face.

"You gon' get caught, you know," she said.

"I'm quick enough."

"Don't look like it the way you finger them peels like they's worms or something."

Martha stopped moving and kept her eyes on her bucket; not her usual response to her friend's taunting. Annise stopped and turned to her. She sighed and then tossed three peels hard into her bucket. "What gon' happen when you get caught? You ever been in the hothouse?" Then she stood up, poured Martha's bucket into her own, and walked across the yard, chickens at her heels. When most of the chickens were in her midst, she scattered the bucket of scraps around the flock.

Martha had never been *inside* the hothouse, but she knew it was a small cabin with no windows or fireplace and would get very hot or cold, depending on the season. Once locked in, water and bread were supposed to be given once a day through a small door. The floor was dirt, and the ceiling was low, too low to stand up. Bill liked the hothouse. If he didn't like the way his day was going, he'd take it out on the men. Bill put old Caleb in there one time for taking an extra piss break. Then he ate Caleb's food. Martha definitely didn't want to end up in the hothouse.

"And you can forget about getting you a man," Annise shouted across the chicken yard. Wesley, who was sharpening an ax under the nearby oak, looked over. Martha's face turned red. She tossed her bucket into the wheelbarrow, pushed it on toward the hog pen, and started pulling out rib bones and overcooked chunks of meat, and then tossed them aside to feed the dogs later on. Behind the wire, the bigger brown and pink hogs stood, watching and snorting.

Annise caught up with her. She said quietly, "I can't stand it . . . You get caught and sold to some other master where they's beat you and lock you up and make you have babies."

Martha cringed, and then she sighed. Ever since she learned about the north, where all people walked free, she's wanted to see it. Live it. There had to be a way to get there. She wondered about the old man hidden in the barn. Would he make it, or would he get caught and beaten?

"Then they sell thems babies," Annise added and threw a large bone into the bucket with a thunk.

"They do not!" Martha huffed. "You just trying make me stay."

Annise shook her head. "Staying here's about best you can do. They's beds and food, and you know Master ain't like them others." Martha thought about her family, how they look out for one another. "Besides, Patrick's here," she added. Annise knew all about Martha's attraction to the man ten years her senior. As silly as it seemed, the feelings were real. "I know I'd never be able to leave my Tom."

The girls worked in silence for a while. Finally, Annise touched Martha's hand, and she looked up. "You can't do it by yourself."

The bluetick dogs that kept the raccoons away were tied to their ropes so they wouldn't run away or fight over the scraps. They wagged their tails anxiously and barked when they saw the girls coming. As they scooped out bones and meat into a happy dog's bowl, the other dog broke its rope and headed for the dish. The two dogs were immediately in a swirling, snapping, and growling cloud of dust.

Martha headed for the dogs, but Annise yelled, "Stop! They bite."

Annise picked up the loose rope and pulled the attacking dog away, and Martha pulled on the other dog's rope. The dog was stronger than Martha and stood his ground.

"Help me with this rope!" she shouted.

Martha grabbed the broken rope. As they pulled the dog out of the fight, it turned and came after Martha. Wesley, who had been watching from where he was assigned to kill chickens, jumped the fence with a pitchfork. The dog growled but stayed back.

The other dog lost interest in the fight and returned to his bowl.

"Quick, get some food for this one's bowl. Thanks, Wesley," said Annise while tying the rope to the hound's rough-hewn shack. Martha dumped some bones in the bowl.

As they walked to their next task, Martha asked, "What should I do?"

"About what?"

"Patrick."

"Do nothing and say nothing," said Annise. "Patrick doesn't

seem to think much of you anyway, pushing you around like that."

Plucking the feathers from a beheaded chicken was another chore they found tedious. The boys seemed to like wielding a hatchet to behead a chicken. Martha covered her eyes like she always did, and Annise laughed at her. The boys chuckled as the chicken ran around bumping into the fences until it collapsed. They tossed the headless feathered carcass over the fence to the girls.

"You got quiet all of a sudden," Annise said.

"I'm going to make Patrick like me and run with me," Martha said, sitting on an overturned feed bucket ripping the feathers out of the headless bird.

In 1833, the Virginia assembly made it a crime for a person to receive a salary for instructing enslaved people how to read and write, and it also made it a criminal offense for "any white person or persons" to "assemble with free negroes or mulattoes, at any school-house, church, meeting-house, or other place for the purpose of instructing such free negroes or mulattoes to read or write."

September 1847, Madison Heights, Virginia

Chapter 2
Quakers Not Being Silent

Frederick slowed the buggy as it neared the circular driveway of Sam Turner's tobacco plantation near Warwick's Spring Hill home. The Quakers were gathering for their traditional service prayers, singing, and meditation. Several members had taken seats on the steps or in chairs that formed a circle with the grand staircase to the mansion. Frederick tethered the horse to a tree and assisted Master Warwick out of the buggy and into a chair with back support. After handing his master the cane, the coachman joined his wife and daughter in the grass outside the circle. They were the only slaves allowed near the Quaker Sunday service.

During Quaker meditation, the Friends bowed their heads or

read silently from their Bibles. After a long period of silence, Sam Turner's wife stood. Her large white bonnet shaded half of her face. The women looked wide-eyed at each other, and the men frowned. Women were not expected to talk at these meetings. Sam glared at her, and redness crept up his neck.

Mrs. Turner said, "As God-fearing Quakers, we must free any people we hold in bondage right now. Today."

An uncomfortable period of silence followed. Most Quakers believed that slaves should be freed. Most thought they should be freed over time, and very few would agree with Mrs. Turner. This division caused the breakup of the Lynchburg congregation, and many Quakers moved up north or out west. Even John Lynch, the founder of the town, left in support of his beliefs. Now, the meetinghouse in Lynchburg was boarded up while slavery continued.

"It isn't right to own another person." Mrs. Turner fumbled in her apron. With shaking hands, she read, "Friend John Greenleaf Whittier from New England wrote in this pamphlet, 'For as long as we recognize the infernal principle that man can hold property in man, God will not hold us guiltless. God will not hold us guiltless,'" she repeated, looking around, attempting to make eye contact with Mrs. Campbell, who looked down and shook her head. A woman near Mrs. Campbell turned and looked at her husband.

She returned to the ragged paper. "To the members of the religious Society of Friends, I would earnestly appeal. Slavery has no redeeming qualities, no feature of benevolence; nothing pure, nothing peaceful, nothing just."

Mrs. Turner's shocked and angry husband pulled her back into a chair.

After a few minutes, Mr. Campbell stood and shook hands with a man sitting next to him. When this happened, the congregation knew that this was the traditional signal that the service was over. This service seemed short today.

Mr. Campbell, glaring at Mrs. Turner, said, "As reasonable and temperate Christians and neighbors in Amherst County, we must allow for our colored to be freed over time. We don't want to have to move north like so many of our brethren."

Most nodded in agreement. The folks gathered knew he did not want to leave graceful southern living that was only possible with slaves. Many of them could not afford to free their slaves.

Sam Turner took his wife by the arm and sent her back to the house. When she hesitated, he clenched his hands and shook his head.

Mr. Campbell shouted over the growing din, "The men should have an after-meeting to discuss further the thought shared today. Meetinghouses have splintered over this issue, and I pray that we can seek spiritual guidance for our actions."

The men looked at each other and moved to a big shade tree.

Mrs. Campbell approached Lucy and Martha and said, "How pretty she looks today in her blue calico dress and matching bonnet," pointing at the girl.

"Oh goodness, thank you, Mrs. Campbell," Lucy said, "but I'm afraid that Martha will let your flattery go to her head."

Martha looked around and shuffled her feet until Mrs. Campbell added, "Your dress is mighty fine also, Lucy." Mrs. Campbell straightened herself and tipping her head back, added, "I'm sure some of the less privileged servants don't understand your finery. My husband thinks your master spoils you with clothes like that."

"Martha, take those chairs into the house," Frederick said.

Martha picked up one chair and went to the back door of Mr. Turner's plantation. She opened the door and carefully carried the chair into the central hallway. Mrs. Turner came to the hall and said, "Thank you."

Her eyes were red, and she held a wet handkerchief. Mrs. Turner grimaced when she pointed toward her dining room.

"Are you OK, Mrs. Turner?" she asked.

"I'm fine."

"I liked what you said today. I want to be free."

"I wish I could make it so. Oh, take this pamphlet and keep it hidden. My husband will burn it if I try to keep it."

Martha took the pamphlet and started to read.

"I didn't know you could read," said Mrs. Turner.

"Everyone in my family can," said Martha. "Ah, but not the baby."

"Who taught you?"

"My white friend's mother when I was a servant. Then I taught my family."

"I'm glad to hear a tutor wasn't hired. John Warwick could get in big trouble."

"He has asked me to teach some of the others, and I like teaching. Master Warwick told us that a law required us not to meet in groups. So, I teach one or two at a time."

Sam Turner said, "My wife was out of place today. She shoots her mouth too much. Colored are inferior and can't support themselves. If we didn't feed and clothe them, they wouldn't know what to do. Owning them is like owning a horse or a smart dog. Also, if you treat them nice, they expect more and do less."

Martha pretended not to hear as she returned to the buggy.

Nearby, waiting in the buggy, Lucy and Frederick sat with stone faces. Martha hissed at Turner's dog remark, and Lucy nudged her quiet with her elbow. Mrs. Turner's pamphlet fell to the floor of the buggy. Martha put one foot over it. Lucy's attention went back to Mr. Turner, and Martha pretended to scratch her leg. John Warwick shook his head and said, "Samuel, they are human beings, and they'd be more helpful if they knew how to read and write. One of my young slaves is better at numbers than anyone I know."

"Virginia has laws against hiring someone to teach colored to read and write," Mr. Turner said, pointing a finger at John Warwick, "as you should well know."

Martha's eyes grew wide, and she quickly grabbed the pamphlet and slid it up the sleeve of her dress.

Warwick added, "They deserve to be freed, and in my view, they are earning their freedom."

Lucy sighed, and Martha relaxed. She was glad that Master Warwick mentioned her skills in math.

Shifting his weight on his cane, Warwick said, "Of course, I know the law. Some of my servants learned while helping as friends of white children on other plantations. Many have taught each other."

Sam Campbell spoke up, "I can't afford to free my slaves. The law requires that slave owners must pay to relocate, says I have to pay to get each one to a free state and buy provisions for a year." Some Quakers were not prepared to make that kind of sacrifice or change their way of life, so they borrowed excuses created by the lawmakers.

Sam continued, "Besides, it's colored thinking they are smart that starts revolts." Then he tipped his hat and stomped away toward his wagon.

Frederick helped Master Warwick into the buggy. "Frederick, take me home before any more negative thoughts foul our hearts and souls."

Frederick shook the reins and said quietly to the horse, "Giddy up, Mr. Turner." Master Warwick chuckled with Martha. Lucy gazed back at the Turner mansion, worried.

The barn, one of six on the plantation, sat at the end of the slave cabins. It was a gathering place for most families and singles once a month on Sunday afternoon and evening. They were expecting a church service with songs and a sermon by their self-anointed preacher dressed in his coachman's uniform and ribbon-wrapped straw hat. They knew his standard message.

The women rocked and sang the hymns as Frederick led with his strong baritone voice. Lucy was glad to see him on his feet and giving a sermon, although she thought this one was shorter. The men hung back, clapping and humming. One of their favorite hymns was "Praise, My Soul, King of Heaven." Frederick had learned it at the Quaker meetings. They sang,

"Praise Him for His grace and favour
To our fathers in distress.
Praise Him still the same for ever,
Slow to chide, and swift to bless
Praise Him! Praise Him!
Glorious in His faithfulness.
Father-like He tends and spares us;
Well our feeble frame He knows.
In His hands He gently bears us,
Rescues us from all our foes.
Praise Him! Praise Him!
Widely as His mercy flows."

After the service, the women gathered to gossip and complained about their men. John Warwick allowed them to live as partners and raise families even though they were not legally allowed to be married. "Oh, you all lucky to have a man around," Nicey said and waved them off.

The boys played their favorite game called willow whip tag. If a young brother ended up with the whip, the older brother would pretend to be caught. This game originated from hearing the hired-out men talking about seeing friends being severely whipped on other plantations.

When Marshall got tired of chasing, he looked around for an easy target among the girls. Mary Elizabeth quickly ducked behind her mother.

Marshall cajoled, "Come on; let's play a game."

Mary Elizabeth, shaking her head, clung to her mother's dress.

Her mother declared, "She ain't as smart as you, but she knows you are holdin' that branch behind your back. If you hit her with it, I'll use it on you."

Marshall whistled a tune as he briskly walked away.

Juda didn't show again for the service, but her boys came to eat. Frederick filled a plate with pork, collards, and corn bread, and then he knocked on her door.

"Juda, you okay?"

She cracked the door. "What you want?"

"I didn't see you today," he said.

"No, you didn't. Now what?" She opened the crack a little more, her hair was tousled, and her face wrinkled from sleep. She looked down at the plate.

Frederick smiled and said, "Maybe you eat and come visit with some folks? Some of the ladies are gathered in a Bible study group under the northern oak."

Juda grabbed the plate, took a bite of corn bread, and looked at Frederick. Then she laughed until she swallowed. "Frederick, what you think I am, stupid?" She set the plate down on a mattress inside and put both hands back on the door. "You go on with your sermons. That's who you be, but don't expect me to show up all doll-eyed and singing songs just because *you* believe they's a God. What lovin' God would treat us this way?"

Frederick sighed, thinking he had failed. Worse, that she might not really care for him. He didn't feel up to preaching to her and only said, "I worry about your soul."

She shook her head, "Frederick, honey, thank you for this food," she said. "But you go on now," and she gently closed the door.

Later that day, while the women gossiped and the boys were rolling hoops, the men gathered in a smaller circle to play cards. On this Sunday, the hired-out people were back. Harold brought rum to share. The still on the Spring Hill Plantation made corn whiskey, but the rum from other plantations was sweeter. The whiskey produced at Spring Hill was stored in barrels made by Anthony, who was the only cooper who could make the barrels.

After a few drinks, the young men were laughing and slapping each other on the back. Frederick took a jug from one man, and he gulped down the liquid several times. Another man grabbed the jug in fear Frederick was going to drop the precious liquid. After he left, they found his Bible on the ground near the jugs.

Harold seemed to like having an audience for his tales. He got their attention when he talked about whippings. You could be whipped for being slow in picking cotton or any other task. A man had tried to run away, but slave catchers were hired and sent after him. They collected their one-hundred-dollar reward and left the slave to his punishment, which was twenty lashes.

"The worst thing I ever saw was a man whipped until his back was bloodred. Then the overseer poured saltwater on his wounds until he passed out."

Caleb, one of the older men, said, "If even I need to piss, I git put in the hothouse. The Bill laughs and eats my food. I think he's tryin' to kill me."

Frederick had not been able to eat much that day. He felt half-heartedly that heaven would be the only way he and his family would ever be free. Lucy had tried to get him to eat more and rest, but he was losing interest in everything, even reading.

When he reached for Lucy under the covers that night, she pushed him away. She said, "I'm trying to sleep, and you been drinkin'."

He put his arm around her and held one breast and forced one leg between hers.

She twisted free and said, "What's a matter with you? Why you want it most nights?"

"I need you."

"No more babies for me."

There are neighborhoods in Baltimore in which the life expectancy is 19 years less than other neighborhoods in the same city.

Washington Post 04/30/2015

October 1848, Slave Quarters, Spring Hill Plantation, Lynchburg, Virginia

Chapter 3

Where There's Smoke There's . . .

It was an autumn evening at dusk, and frost could be expected by morning. The cabin windows glowed from candles and fireplaces burning. Dinners were being prepared over open fires, and the embers would keep the cabin warm throughout the night.

The men, women, and any children over six returned from the fields tired, dirty, and hungry. Women with babies spent the day looking after them.

Many were glad to settle in with their families. Suddenly, on the road, Patrick cried out, "Fire!"

Within seconds, there was a chorus of loud voices repeating the dreaded word. People poured into the center road. Sparks and flames flew from the roof of Patrick's cabin. The danger of fires was why the big house had a separate cooking cabin. Sparks from a fireplace in one of their cabins could easily start a roof fire and spread. The cabins were made with cheap clapboard as were the fireplaces. The units were too close.

Patrick's aging mother started this fire with her excessive stirring of the embers caused by her tremor. Patrick had been unable to convince her to let him do the cooking.

What followed was a well-orchestrated bucket brigade. Jack showed up, riding his unsaddled horse to observe. The cabins had been built close together to save farmland, so the community had anticipated fires like this one. Luckily, Jack and Bill had made them practice in the past. Men and women formed a line passing full buckets of water. A second line of children returned the empty buckets to the well. Patrick ran from the barn with their only ladder and climbed to reach the roof. They passed buckets up to him, who chucked water onto the flames. Below him in the burning cabin, his mother and Martha were moving the table and benches out to the road. They also threw water on the nearby cabins.

Wesley asked, "Will we form a line to save Bill and Juda's cabins from the fire?"

Some were murmuring in agreement, then Frederick said, "Jesus would, and so will we."

"Fire's out," shouted Patrick.

"Let us pray. Thank you, God. No one was hurt, and no cabins caught fire. We Patrick always help our neighbors," Frederick said.

Some of the older boys picked up full buckets and threw water at one another. When they tired of chasing the others, they looked for the girls. They were disappointed that the girls had disappeared.

Patrick went inside his cabin, where acrid smoke smell filled the air. Looking through the gaping hole, he saw stars. The dirt floor was now slick mud, and a stream was flowing from the fireplace around a soaked mattress and out the front door. The shirt he took from a nail had turned black. It would take weeks to clean and repair his cabin after working all day. "What will we do?" Patrick looked at the fireplace and grimaced.

Martha shook her head. "Why don't we have a separate cooking cabin like the big house? It could be shared."

Lucy laughed her off. "We don't get along good enough to share."

"Was anyone hurt?" asked John Warwick, leaning on his cane.

Jack said, "No sir."

"I'll feed Patrick and his mother," said Lucy.

"They can stay in the servant's quarters in my house until their cabin is repaired," Master Warwick said, and added, "Jack, assign someone to work with Patrick and free Patrick from the fields until he can move back."

"Yes sir," Jack said.

"Thank you, Master Warwick," said Patrick.

"I can't live like this much longer," whispered Martha to Annise.

Couples were not entitled to live under the same roof, as each spouse could have a different owner, miles apart. All slaves dealt with the threat of forcible separation; untold numbers experienced it first-hand.

New York Times 08/02/2011

October 1848, Downtown, Lynchburg, Virginia

Chapter 4
Two Kinds of Markets

Lucy and Martha waited while Master Warwick met with his lawyer. The door had been left ajar, and Martha was trying to see what the man's office looked like.

Mr. Dillard was smacking one of his fists into his other hand and shouting, "You can't put seventy-five free colored on the streets of Lynchburg. People here think free colored will organize and start a rebellion. It has happened in other towns and on the islands, and many folks think it will happen here. We have almost one thousand free colored that have moved here from Alabama and South Carolina." The man's reflection moved back and forth across the room as he paced. "Under Virginia manumission laws, if you were to free them, you would have to arrange for them to go to Liberia in

Africa or a free state."

Martha looked at her mother and mouthed the word "Africa." Lucy waved for her daughter to move away from the door.

The waiting area outside Mr. Dillard's office was far nicer than their furniture in the cabin. The big pillows also made this a comfortable place to sit. A bay window behind the couch allowed for a full view of the busy street below where the trees were in full colors of red, yellow, and orange. The waiting room was now eerily quiet except for Lucy's knitting needles and the ticking of the grandfather clock.

"You want to do something Christian?" Dillard said. "Sell your slaves before you die and give the money to charity."

Martha froze in her seat, sharing a horrified stare with her mother. The silence that followed lasted a long time before Master Warwick came out. When he did, Lucy got to her feet and handed him his cane.

As they were leaving, Mr. Dillard said, "As you wish, John."

The market in Lynchburg was out in the open by the river, with many sellers under tents. The sour scent of the horses and mules traveled farther on a hot day like this one, and it mixed with the smell of fresh melons cut open and displayed for passersby to smell the sweetness. Lucy and Martha carried baskets through the market as negotiations between vendors and buyers rang loud with a din much like everyone talking over each other during dinner in their small cabin. The tents, strung with sheets, provided cool shade for many of the sellers. Colored vendors stood in the hot afternoon sun, wiping sweat from their cheeks as they hawked apples, melons, and other produce.

Lucy stopped in front of the apples and nudged Martha. "Here, fill your basket halfway with apples so that we have enough for everyone." Martha nodded and started counting apples into her basket. Glad to get the business, the black man smiled and nodded to Lucy before she moved down the walkway toward the beans. Mr. Moon was a free man who fed his family by collecting and selling dropped apples from the orchard of his former master.

"Young lady," a woman said, shaking her head and tapping Martha on the hand. "What you want these rotten drops for?" Martha looked up, confused. They'd always purchased apples from Mr. Moon, and none were ever rotten. She looked into the white woman's basket where six bright, shiny reds lined the bottom. No bruises. Then the woman pointed to a farmer down the row with fresh red apples lined up on his cart under a tent. His apples looked better, maybe even juicier, Martha thought, and she wondered if she should trade them out.

Lucy cut in, "I'm sorry, ma'am, but my daughter and I always buy Mr. Moon's apples." The woman stepped back, seemingly shocked. The man quickly looked down and busied himself straightening a row of his fruit. "They may be leftovers, but we're just fine with them, thank you." Lucy paid the man. "Good day, Aron," she said.

"Yes," he said, nodding. "Good day to you, Miss Lucy. Thank you." He took the money, wiped his brow, and nodded again.

The woman joined her friend in the shade under a nearby tent. "Would you look at those two?" she said.

Her friend adjusted her spectacles and looked at Martha, then winced at Lucy. "Well . . ." she said. Then she fanned her face and said over the crowd, "That nigga's as fair as you."

The first woman huffed. "What is this town coming to?"

Lucy and Martha made their way past the catty pair, keeping their gazes low. The woman's friend nodded as John Warwick meandered by with his cane. Then she said aloud, "Looks like she's from that Quaker plantation. I hear tell that old Quaker likes messing with his women," and then they laughed. Martha turned around at them to make an ugly face and then quickly turned back.

Wesley and Frederick Jr. slowed the wagons loaded with tobacco. The wagons were rigged so that the tobacco leaves, tied to long sticks, could hang across in rows. They stopped in front of a long, low barn. Without an active railroad through town, commerce was dependent on the James River Kanawha Canal for the transportation of goods, and this barn was on the canal. The boys lifted each stick together and moved it onto large pegs inside the barn to continue drying.

The textile tables were busy with the unfolding and refolding of linens and fabrics. Lucy was tasked to select materials supplied to all of the families. Then the women gathered twice a year to make clothes. Seventy-five people required a lot of fabric. Master Warwick, already tired, had settled onto a row of crates set up as a bench. He leaned forward onto his cane, guarded the produce baskets, and watched Lucy work her magic. She'd already negotiated the best price for material for the men's trousers. Nearby, two young women manned a table while their mother strung freshly dyed fabrics on a pole behind them. Lucy cleared her throat, and the woman tucked a dirty lock of blond hair behind her ear and turned. Lucy fumbled with a colorful scarf she'd been knitting for the past few weeks. The woman stood and smiled. She reached under the girls' table for a clean stack of white fabrics and set it on top of the other piles. Lucy nodded and handed the scarf to the woman who looked it over, smiled, and then placed two new rolls of yarn on top of the pile.

Negotiations complete, Lucy picked up the two stacks of fabrics and rolled them up. She put the white roll over Martha's shoulder and the colored roll on her own. "Where are we, Martha?" Martha did the math, held up four fingers, and then quickly put them away. Lucy now knew exactly how much she had left over after her creative bargaining and trade to bring some prettier fabrics back for the ladies.

After the market, Frederick stopped the buggy at the railroad where a man in uniform stood at the door of a big train car. Frederick Jr. and Wesley halted their wagons behind them. The conductor called out, "I have some crates for you, Mr. Warwick."

John Warwick limped with his cane over to the train car with Frederick and said, "What do you have for me? I wasn't expecting anything." He was moving slower today.

"I'll have to open one to see. The crates are marked fragile," said the conductor.

"How many crates are there?" said Warwick.

"Just two, and they are heavy."

"Frederick, climb up there and open one. I want to know what's in them," said Warwick. Frederick handed Master Warwick a plate and said, "Where is havi land?"

Warwick frowned and raised his hand to his cheek. "Haviland china is some of the best and most famous in the world, made in France. My wife must have ordered these before she died."

"They are paid for," said the conductor.

"Put this dish back, Frederick, and have the boys move the crates to the supply wagon and secure them. They have come a long way without being broken."

From the back of the buggy, Lucy watched the old man teetering in the distance with Frederick at his side. She shook her head and mumbled, "That man gets more brittle with every sunset."

"Mm-hmm," Martha agreed. "He sure ain't messin' with his girls," she said, fanning herself like the catty woman from earlier.

Lucy said, "Hush, now," and slapped Martha on the leg.

As Frederick helped his master into the buggy, Martha gazed out the window. Then turning to her mother, she asked, "How did Mr. Moon get two names? He has a last name. Why don't we have a last name?" Master Warwick moaned, and Lucy wondered if the old man had heard her daughter's question, then figured he didn't. She leaned over to Martha.

"Only free people have last names," Lucy whispered. "Now, stop asking so many questions!"

As the buggy was leaving the market area, a gathering came into view. A colored man, woman, and young girl were standing on a platform, naked and shaking. A couple of men were walking around the family, poking and prodding with sticks. A small crowd surrounded the action.

"What are they doing?" Martha asked.

The buggy stopped in the square, and Lucy put her hand over her daughter's eyes. When Martha protested, Frederick, from the coachman's perch, turned and said, "Let her watch. She needs to know." Lucy dropped her hand and held Martha around the waist, close to her.

A man picked up the young girl and said, "I'll take this one. You are asking a hundred dollars, but I'll pay only fifty." The girl was squirming and squealed for her momma. Martha cringed. The woman yelled at the man and reached for her daughter, but the other man pushed her to her knees.

"Make it seventy-five, and she's yours," said the high-hat auctioneer from his corner of the platform. Shifting the squirming girl to his other arm, he nodded consent and said, "If you didn't oil these folks so much, they would be easier to handle."

"What's the delay?" asked Warwick.

"A wagon is blocking the street," Frederick said.

The older woman pleaded, "No. Take me! Take me too."

The black man, whose hands were tied, started toward the young girl, but then he saw the other man with a knife standing behind his woman. He froze, and in one quick move, the man sliced off part of her right ear.

"Don't you move," he threatened.

The woman wailed, bright red blood ran down her shoulder and dripped to the floor. Martha gasped and gripped the side of the buggy so tightly her knuckles turned white. Lucy whimpered. Frederick stared straight-ahead.

"I'll take him for the five hundred you posted," shouted a tall man in the crowd, and the auctioneer dragged the slave from the platform. Martha looked back at the young girl in time to see her in the back of a wagon with the driver tightening a rope around her chest. She'd been gagged, her face wet with tears and sweat. Martha thought of her daddy and knew that he wouldn't have been any stronger than the bound man against those men and their weapons and chains. The helplessness of it all nauseated her.

The buggy began to move, and Lucy said, "Look straight-ahead," then her face went to stone. It wasn't to control what her daughter saw, but more to give her a better option than watching the horror, and Martha sensed it by the defeat in her mother's voice. She turned forward, but she didn't look straight-ahead. Instead, she looked at Master Warwick with heated anger. Why did he let this happen? He could have bought that family and brought them home, and they'd still be together, she thought.

John Warwick sat quietly, looking down at his shoes with a defeated look. He used to buy slaves for the very reason of keeping families together, but his olive branch had been shut down ever since the locals started going out of their way to outbid him. He hadn't been able to save anyone from the local auctions for a long time. He was helpless. He sighed, leaned forward, and gripped Frederick's shoulder for a long moment. Then he looked straight-ahead as well.

"You could have got them," Martha said in a nasty tone.

"Martha!" her mother said.

"Mrs. Turner was right," Martha continued. "Nobody should own nobody."

Lucy put her hand over Martha's mouth, squeezed, and said, "I'm sorry, Master Warwick."

"No, no, Lucy," he said. "She's right." He looked straight at Martha and said, "People should not own anyone."

Martha huffed and turned away from him and her mother's hold. John Warwick closed his eyes and said, "No one."

A few minutes down the road, John Warwick sighed, laid his head on Lucy's shoulder, and fell asleep.

Blacks face the possibility of life servitude. The General Assembly of Virginia decides that any child born to an enslaved woman will also be a slave regardless of the color of the father.

1662, Virginia Law

March 1848, Spring Hill Plantation, Virginia

Chapter 5
Death and Life

John Warwick got up from his bed and reached for his cane. Moving across the room, he tripped on the rug and fell hard onto the broad plank floor. Lucy heard the heavy sound and hurried up the stairs to his room. His cane was askew by the dresser, and the Oriental rug was rumpled. She got on her knees next to him. He placed a hand on her shoulder and tried to get up, only to fall again, moaning.

"I'll get help." Lucy ran down the stairs. At the kitchen house, Martha stirred the chicken broth while Frederick and Frederick Jr. waited to serve dinner. "Master Warwick has fallen and needs your help."

Frederick and Frederick Jr. raced toward the back door with Lucy and Martha close on their heels.

In Master Warwick's bedroom, the men lifted him from the floor despite his painful moans. They placed him gently in his bed, and he rolled to one side.

"Is he okay?" Martha whispered.

"I hope so. Frederick Jr., go tell Wesley to fetch Dr. Patteson," Lucy said.

"Martha, I want you to stay and help. Frederick, bring me some chicken broth from the kitchen," said Lucy in her take-charge mode.

A few minutes later, they heard Wesley's horse galloping away. Dr. Patteson lived twenty miles away, which meant that Lucy was in charge of her master's health, possibly through the night.

Lucy washed his face with a cloth and tried to get him to take some tea. "Where does it hurt, Master Warwick?"

"In my hip."

"Do you want your box of herbs?" Martha asked.

"Not until Dr. Patteson gets here. He will know which ones are best for Master Warwick."

"It hurts too much to sit up. Maybe just prop me up a little," said Master Warwick.

Lucy handed Martha a chamber pot. "Take this to the privy and bring it back clean."

It felt good to be able to help, but Martha didn't like this particular task. She started down the back stairs and realized that even with a lid, the mess in the pot could overflow if she wasn't extra careful. She put the pot down to get the back door open, and again at the privy door, where a blast of putrid air assailed her as she entered. Grimacing, she lifted the lid on the seat box where the waste she saw in the bottom had been cooking and marinating from the heat of the sun. "Why didn't Momma ask one of my brothers to do this?" she complained in the fading light of the privy.

In the morning, Lucy tried to move Warwick so he could eat, but he moaned so much that she stopped.

Dr. Patteson came into the bedroom, breathless, and asked, "What happened, John?"

"I tripped and fell. My left hip hurts a lot, and I haven't been able to sleep. Bless Lucy. She's taking good care of me."

"Let's have a look at you," Dr. Patteson said, putting his hand on Master Warwick's forehead. "He has a slight fever." He placed a tube on Warwick's chest and held one end of the tube to his ear. He pulled the sheet back and moved Warwick's right leg bending it at the knee. When he tried to bend his left leg, Warwick let out a deep-throated moan.

"I want to get you out of bed, John, and see how you do," said Dr. Patteson.

Dr. Patteson put his arm around Master Warwick and asked him to put his legs over the edge of the bed. When Master Warwick tried to stand on his own, he almost passed out and fell back on the bed.

"His heart is pounding, which is a reaction to the pain. Give him this medicine whenever he feels pain and try to get him to eat. The laudanum will help him sleep. I'm afraid his hip is broken, and there is little we can do. Moving his good leg and arms will help his circulation. Keep people away so he can rest," said Dr. Patteson.

"Thank you, Dr. Patteson. I'll do as you say," said Lucy as he left the room.

Lucy said gently, "I'm going to roll you on your side so that I can wash you." When she moved him to his side, he moaned loudly.

People began gathering at the back porch steps to find out what happened. Patrick was the first to inquire. He started up the steps to the back entrance, and Martha stopped him by placing a broom handle across the railings.

"I want to check on Master Warwick," Patrick said, growling. He placed his hands on the broom handle.

He bent the broom handle like a bow, and Martha saw the muscles in his arms ripple. Frowning at him, she said, "If you don't break the broom, I'll let you in."

Patrick let out his breath, slipped past Martha, and went up the back stairs quietly. He stopped in the doorway, and Lucy shook her head. Patrick saw that Warwick was sleeping, so he returned to the back door.

"Is he going to be okay?" Patrick asked more patiently this time.

"We won't know for a while," said Martha.

"What happened to him?" said Annise.

"Dr. Patteson thinks he broke his hip," replied Martha.

"That is bad news. I know people who broke a hip, and it wasn't long before they got very sick," said Annise.

"Is that true?" asked Martha, looking at her friend with eyes beginning to water.

"I have heard the same thing from other folks," commented Patrick.

Frederick Jr. took over from Martha, and several slaves had gathered at the back porch, trying to find out what happened.

"I heard he fell down the steps," one woman said.

They talked too fast for Frederick Jr. to get a word in until one man shouted over the din, "I heard Warwick got shot."

This seemed to get their attention, and finally, Frederick Jr. was able to speak. "No no no. He fell and hurt his hip." He did his best to explain that he had fallen and was now resting.

A woman stepped forward, fidgeting with her hands. "What will happen to us if he, you know . . ." the woman's voice trailed off. No one could answer her. By noon, someone from almost every family had stopped to see how he was doing.

Lucy stayed with her master for seven days and nights. He was having difficulty sleeping because when he coughed, his hip hurt, and that kept him awake. Swallowing became difficult, and Lucy could not get him to eat anything. It was all she could do to give him a spoon of laudanum and some tea.

The work on the plantation continued, though quiet. Many didn't want to speculate on Warwick's outcome and what could happen to them if he died. Would they be passed on to another Warwick in another town? Would families be split up and sold? Were they headed for the auction block? Those who had been to or came from other plantations knew about the abuse, the rape, and the torture at the hands of sadistic men. Spring Hill didn't see as much hatred as elsewhere. They began praying for their master to get well. In fact, so many slaves were visiting Frederick's cabin for guidance in prayer that he sat out nightly on the front porch steps of the big house to be available. They kneeled in a circle, closed their eyes, and held hands. Their mouths moved quietly to themselves, promising anything they could think of to appease the Lord and save their master from death.

Warwick's condition declined quickly once he stopped eating. At one point, he woke, saw Lucy sharing his pillow, and smiled, only to begin coughing in an uncontrollable fit that woke her.

Martha appeared in the doorway. "Mama," she said. She ran to Warwick's bedside but could only watch. She was helpless.

"Master John, please relax," Lucy said.

He shook his head, swallowed some cold tea that she held to his lips, and took a long, slow breath. He coughed again into his sheet, leaving a fairly large spot of blood. "Lucy, I think it is time," he said in a tight voice. "I need to talk to Frederick."

She sent Martha to get her father. "You can't go yet," she begged.

"We need you here, Master John."

"Please take care of my son, will you?"

Outside, Martha found Frederick in the barn and screamed at him to come quickly. He didn't need to ask. They sprinted back to the house, which seemed miles away, rushed up the stairs, and approached the master's quarters. Martha ran inside, but Frederick hesitated outside the door. He closed his eyes and took a breath.

"No!" Martha screamed as Frederick entered the room.

Master Warwick lay still in his bed, blood on parts of the sheet and his pillow. Lucy shook her head and sobbed from the chair beside the bed.

"I'm sorry, Frederick," she said. He approached the bed and put his arm around her. Then he stared at John Warwick, and his face paled. "He tried to tell you in time. I'm so sorry!" Lucy sobbed harder, and Martha took her hand, never imagining that she'd be comforting her mother.

Frederick began mumbling as if in shock. ". . . good man . . . was righteous . . ."

Lucy took a deep breath and calmed herself; then she stood up. She turned his face to hers. "I am so sorry, Frederick." Lucy shook her head. "He wanted to say good-bye . . . your father."

Frederick winced and stepped back from her. He shook his head and looked over at the dead man's body as if he had been a stranger. He touched his own cheek, fingers moving over his light skin.

"He wanted to tell you himself," she continued.

"No." Frederick backed up a few more steps. "How I supposed to believe what you say when this man is dead?" He shook his head again. "No," he repeated and ran out of the room.

The news of John Warwick's death spread quickly through the plantation, as did the news of Frederick's paternity, though many had already guessed by the special treatment he and his family received, and by the lighter color of his skin. But Frederick had been told a different story growing up about his father dying before his birth. Nicey and Caleb, having been around when Frederick was born, along with his mother, took the liberty of feeding the boy many tales meant to keep his birth father a secret. Frederick took those bits and pieces, and he imagined a strong, respectable father, a man who believed in God and heaven and hope for a better future. Frederick's vision, having worked just fine for the entirety of his life, was sound. And while John Warwick had always favored Frederick and his family, he was still a slave owner. And no slave wants a slave owner for a father.

The next evening, Frederick had news and asked his family to stand for prayer. "Most merciful God, you have taken our master from us, and while that leaves us not knowing what tomorrow will bring, thank you, God, for your grace in keeping us together for another season. Whatever happens, we will follow your way. Amen."

"Amen," they said and then sat down to eat. The group ate quietly for a while before Martha spoke up. "One season is not that long," she said.

"We'll know more after the harvest," Frederick replied.

It should have been enough information, but thirteen-year-old Martha, now showing the signs of womanhood, harbored stronger urges to run.

"What will happen when they're done with us?" Martha said, her eyes fierce.

"Martha," her mother began.

"You don't know," Martha shouted. "No one knows."

The rules were still the same. Show up for work at seven and work until six. Frederick's family would still work in the big house and serve Dr. Patteson when he visited. His son Rubin was going to live there as an overseer replacing Bill. Rubin was to be treated like Master Warwick had been. Lucy and Martha were going to be in the fields except when Warwick's brother's family came or when Dr. Patteson had multiple guests. Frederick's family got little rest on weekends. On weekdays, they were back in the fields.

Martha now worked seven days a week, losing Sunday afternoons and sometimes her weekday evenings, and leaving her so tired that she had no time to herself. Her itch to run was stronger than ever.

One night, she snuck out of the cabin and into Master Warwick's study. There, she swiped a couple of pens and some paper, slipped out the back way, and then stashed them under a couple of shingles on the roof of the kitchen house.

Dr. Patteson called on Harold Sims seeking to continue John Warwick's arrangement with him of hiring out some of his slaves. Mr. Sims didn't invite him inside his home but talked to him standing on his front porch.

"I don't want free colored talkin' to my colored."

"They don't know they are free."

"They'd be the only ones who don't know. All my neighbors know, and some of my slaves overheard people talkin'. You don't have to stick by the will. Folks think you're making a big mistake and that you should not keep those people here," Harold said.

"The will said to take them after the crops are in," Dr. Patteson said. "I gave my word."

"He's dead. Your word to him don't matter now."

"I signed court documents."

"Who reads that crap?" Harold Sims held his head high. It was apparent he had no intention of helping Patteson—only to make his job more difficult.

"Good day, Mr. Sims." Patteson turned to leave. Sims stepped in front of him, blocking his way to the steps.

"Where'd you bury him?"

Patteson sighed, but he did not tell. No one needed to be desecrating a decent man's grave. "Good day, Sims," he repeated and stepped around the man.

"People want to know. They have a right to know!"

That all slaves so set free . . . shall respectively be supported and maintained by the person so liberating them, or by his or her estate. Every African American freed on or after May 1, 1806, was required to leave the state within a year of manumission or risk being re-enslaved.

Virginia Law (1806)

November 1848, Spring Hill Plantation

Chapter 6
Am I Free Yet?

The harvest was complete, and thanks to the likes of Harold Sims for spreading the malicious word, Patteson's attempt to sell to Warwick's regular buyers was met with avoidance and disdain. The harvest of tobacco had to be carted to nearby towns and sold late to buyers who had already acquired their stock. However, some bought anyway, for a pretty penny less. Still, it was done, and the harvest celebration was planned to include a sermon along with a feast of roast hog for that evening.

Another Conestoga wagon rattled to a stop in the circle in front of the big house. A tall man in a dusty green shirt with a red bandana around his neck hopped down and untied the two horses. A younger man secured the wheels with rocks. Then they hopped on the horses and rode away. The wagons had been showing up for days. This was the fourth to arrive, and various people were making claims to their purpose. Some thought that John Warwick's brother was moving into the big house and would take over the plantation. Others believed that the land had been sold and that the slaves would be next, auctioned off one by one, with no consideration to family. Martha was certain, that with her hips and fair skin, she'd be sold as a breeder, and that one of those wagons would take her to her misery.

All the more reason to run.

Running north wasn't going to be easy. She would miss her family, but it shouldn't take long to get a job, she believed. Then she could save and later buy her family's freedom. Still, getting away was her priority, and she knew she couldn't do it alone. She would have to step up her plan.

Martha rapped on the door of Patrick's cabin, and he shouted for her to come in. After the fire, the men had helped him rebuild. Martha expected, with his mother now passed away and his grieving and all, that the place would be a mess. It wasn't. His belongings were cleared, and his clothing hung neatly on hooks.

"Martha?" Patrick said, surprised to see her. She could feel his eyes on her, which is precisely why she wore the most fitting dress her mother had.

"Patrick, I need to ask you something."

He stepped forward and met her in the middle of the room . . . so close that she could smell the soap on his skin, but he did not invite her to sit. "What is it?" he said. Straight to the point. This was going to be harder than she thought. Martha fumbled with the tie on the back of her dress and looked down at the floor. Something about him always made her feel small.

"We been friends as long as I can remember, right?" she started.

"I guess so, yea," he said.

"Patrick, I'm scared."

He stepped back slightly, and she looked up at him. "Well, what are you afraid of?"

"Those wagons. No one knows why they're here," she said. Patrick stood there. "What if they sell us off?" She touched his arm. "What if . . ." and her voice trailed off. Shaking, she couldn't say what she was thinking. She wanted Patrick to hold her, but instead, he backed away again and looked at the door.

"We don't know what the wagons are here for," he said, then he scratched his head. "I guess we'll find out soon. They can't sit there forever." Martha found no comfort in his words, and she sighed. Patrick looked at the door again and then put his arm around her shoulders. "Look, Martha. Why don't you forget about the wagons and go to the celebration? Try to enjoy the food and music."

"Are you going?"

"Yes," he answered, almost too quickly. Then he led her to the door and opened it. "I'll be there. Then we'll hear what's going to happen to us."

As Martha walked away down the path, she imagined them building their own cabin in the woods up north. She'd teach him to read right away so he could get a job, and she'd look for work with children. Teaching maybe. Martha was lost in her thoughts when she passed a familiar face whom she hadn't seen for almost a year. A girl. Pleasant had been hired out to a family in town to take care of their two children, and now she was back. Martha hadn't noticed until now. What she did notice was that Pleasant too had blossomed into a woman. And a handsome one at that. This didn't matter much to Martha really, being that she herself knew how to read and write while most of the other slaves were just learning. Besides, she and Patrick would be gone soon enough.

Then Martha began to have second thoughts. *What if I miss my family more than I realize? I do love them, but won't they be hurt or worry about me?* She wondered if she should tell her mother her plans, then decided not to, as her mother would surely have her watched by her brothers. *I will miss my best friend.*

As Martha came into view of the celebration being set up, her thoughts turned back to Patrick. *Just wait until he sees what I have for him.*

Martha went to the gathering with Annise and Thomas, her boyfriend, but she had no desire to join them in singing and dancing. She wondered how people could carry on as such. Hadn't everyone seen the wagons? Watching Annise dancing, she wondered if they'd be sold to the same owner. Would they have their babies together? Martha knew that wasn't going to happen to her. She saw Patrick sitting by the fire, eating a rib, pork fat dripping down his chin. Then she ran off and snuck behind the kitchen house when no one was looking. There, under a feed bucket held down by a rock, she pulled out the papers she'd made for Patrick. All they had to do was get out of Virginia with these papers, and they'd be free. She rolled them up, tucked them under her arm, and snuck back to the celebration.

As Martha approached the fire, she had every intention to sit down on the rock next to Patrick and show him the wonderful papers that would grant them a lifetime of good fortune. She imagined that he'd jump up and hug her tightly. Then he'd ask her when they would leave. She intended as soon as possible, perhaps later that night, when everyone was asleep. And though Patrick hadn't smiled much lately, what with his mama dying and all, Martha believed that he'd smile at this. But when she reached his side of the fire, she found Pleasant settling down on her rock. Sitting upright in a pale pink dress and draped in a silky shawl, obviously a gift from the people she had worked for, Pleasant had Patrick's full attention. Martha stomped her foot and huffed. Then she approached Patrick anyway.

"Here, Patrick," she said. "I have something for you." She flashed the rolled papers for him to see but didn't hand them to him. She needed to talk to him alone. No one else needed to know about her plans—especially not Pleasant. It was then that she noticed the book on Pleasant's lap. She'd been reading to Patrick! Martha's face grew red. Not only did the girl come back looking like some angel from God's heaven, but she was blessed with the words too?

"What is it, Martha?" he said. Pleasant said hello. Around the corner, on the makeshift stage, Master Patteson was calling people to gather around.

"Patrick was telling me about you today. Would you like to join us?"

"No," Martha said. The idea that Pleasant felt the need to invite her to sit at a campfire that Martha would have joined on her own unnerved her. And why were they talking about her, she wondered. "Patrick, I need to talk to you." She looked around, unaware of the people moving toward the stage, and then whispered, "Privately."

"I think Dr. Patteson is about to tell us something, Martha. Can we talk after?"

"Yes," Pleasant added, "Surely you can talk after," and she stood to follow the others.

Martha screamed in frustration, which took Patrick and Pleasant by surprise. Then she ran into the nearby woods. Patrick chased her until they both tired and fell into the leaves beneath the grand oaks, heaving. They took a couple of minutes to catch their breath.

"What is with you, Martha? What's so important?"

Martha sighed and handed him the papers. "I made these for you." He unrolled the pages and looked at the writing as if he were reading. "They going to sell us, Patrick. That's what the wagons are for. I don't want to be sold."

Patrick tried to make sense of the writing. He recognized his name, Patrick, on the first page and in various places on the other pages.

"They are free papers," Martha explained, "for you."

He looked up from the paper. "What you mean?"

"We can go! We can run north and be free!"

Patrick wrinkled his face in disgust and shook his head. "Are you crazy? What you going to do when you get caught? They will hang you, Martha. They'll hang *me*!"

"We can go tonight, Patrick, when everyone's asleep, and be far up the road before first light."

"This is stupid," he said, and he ripped the pages in half. Martha screamed and tried to grab them back, but Patrick kept ripping them. "I don't want to be hanged because you made these stupid papers." He looked at Martha and expected her to cry, but then he remembered that she was no longer the little girl he used to know.

Martha stood up and brushed the dirt and leaves off her dress. "I'm going," she said, her tone defiant. She continued to brush the backside of her dress. "I'll go without you."

Patrick stood up and grabbed her hand. "Oh, Martha," he said, and he pulled her in to hold her. She leaned her head against his warm chest and sobbed. In the distance, they heard screaming. Everyone was screaming!

Lucy had spent the afternoon preparing vegetables for the celebration and was gathering them in baskets, but stopped upon seeing Frederick walk in. They locked eyes as Frederick held open the door and waved off the children, saying, "I need to talk to your mama."

They hopped out and plopped down next to the outside step, the youngest tottering in circles around his sister.

"What is it, Frederick?"

"You gonna need to sit down for this, Lucy," he said.

"I need to get these vegetables to the bonfire is what I need. What you—"

"Just sit!" Frederick's voice raised. He couldn't contain his excitement any longer. When Lucy sat down, he grabbed the back of an empty chair with both hands and blurted out, "The old man did it! He did it, Lucy!"

"What did he do?" Normally, Lucy would have dismissed Frederick for his silliness, but she'd seen the wagons arriving one by one. People had been talking. They knew something was about to happen. They just didn't know exactly what it was.

"We are free!"

Now Lucy waved him off. "Talking free. You don't know what you're saying."

Frederick moved around the table and kneeled in front of her. He took her hand and held it to his cheek. "I am as serious as I can be. You and me and the children. We are all free."

Lucy jumped out of her chair. "Husband, you better not be telling me stories." Frederick stood, grinning more so than she'd ever seen. He stomped his foot and stood at attention.

"*Manumitted and set free*. It's what Master Warwick's will say."

Lucy covered her mouth with both hands and screamed as quietly as she could. Frederick held open his arms, and she ran to him and hugged him so hard he about lost his breath. "I don't believe it!" she said. She let Frederick go and stood back. "No wonder Master Patteson has been at the house so much." She beamed. "And those wagons. I knew there was something." Lucy paced the floor. "I knew there was something." Then, after a few moments, her mood shifted. The wagons meant that they were leaving. "Where are we going to go, Frederick? What will we do?" Frederick caught her by the arm.

He told her that Master Warwick arranged for the families to travel north and settle in the free state of Indiana.

"Indiana? How far is Indiana?" she said, and Frederick just shrugged.

"A long way is what I know. And it's cold there too," he said. Lucy looked around the cabin. She'd lived here as long as she could remember. All of her children were born here.

"There's more," Frederick said. He told her that he was given the option to stay on the plantation if he wanted to, he and his family. They could work the house field for food, and he'd have some reward payments from Master Warwick to keep them going, but they would not be free.

Lucy thought for a moment and then looked hopeful. "If we stay, we can add a room onto the cabin," she said. With all the children, she'd always wanted a little more space. "We could build our own cookhouse!"

"I suppose," Frederick said, his blood pumping. He hadn't seen his wife this excited in a long time.

"I could make clothing and sell at the market." She turned to Frederick. "Would you drive for Dr. Patteson or Master Rubin? What work would you do?"

"I don't know."

She rattled on. "You could start your own church. With our own cookhouse, Nicey and I could . . ." and then Lucy's voice trailed off. She realized that even if they stayed, his congregation, her best friend, and everyone she knew would be gone. Frederick realized it too, and Lucy watched his expression change from wonder to concern

"Frederick . . ." she said, but it was too late. He'd already stood up and walked out the door.

Martha and Patrick found no one around the fire, so they headed for the gathering.

"Come on, Martha," Patrick said as he picked up his pace. From what he could see—people laughing and hugging and dancing—something joyous had happened. As they neared the group, Pleasant appeared, smiling and skipped toward Patrick.

"Did you hear it, Patrick?" She stopped in front of him and grabbed both of his hands. Martha stopped in her tracks. "We are free! No more slaves. We are free!"

"What?" he said.

"Master Warwick freed us in his will!" Pleasant ran to Martha and grabbed her hands. Dancing in a circle, she said, "Isn't it wonderful, Martha? We all have papers!"

Martha was stunned. Were they *really* free? People in the gathering began singing altogether, more people than ever sang at Frederick's services. Patrick turned to talk to a man in the crowd, and Martha's head began to spin. It seemed so unreal. Then she thought of Frederick in Juda's cabin. If it's true, then maybe he was only notifying her of the news. That's all. When she heard Patrick's voice again, she turned to him.

"Oh, Pleasant, it's true!" he said. Pleasant laughed and touched his face. Then he grabbed her around the waist and swung her in a circle. She howled with joy, and when he set her back on the ground, he kissed her.

In the cabin, Martha headed straight for the ladder to her loft bed. She fell back into the hay, stared up at the rafters, and cried quietly to herself until long after the singing stopped. Martha's idea of freedom had included Patrick, the two of them alone, together, but that was no longer an option. Now she can stay with her family, but she'll still have to see Patrick and Pleasant together all the time. At least she won't have to work in the fields anymore. She won't have to serve in the big house or shovel slop for the pigs any longer. Or would she? Would they even have animals? Master Warwick and Dr. Patteson always provided most of the food. What would they eat now? Would they stay on the plantation, and if not, where would they go? She had so many questions. What does freedom even look like?

Martha was so busy with her thoughts that she didn't hear Lucy enter and sit down at the table.

Lucy's mind raced with the dangers of traveling in unprotected wagons as such. There would be lots of walking that Frederick would have to suffer. If one of them were to get sick, would she have enough dried herbs for remedies? She worried that pattyrollers could grab any one of them or their kids and drag them off to be sold, and there was nothing they could do as long as Dr. Patteson held their papers. There was no other proof, really. Lucy shivered. A draft moved its way through the cabin, and she pictured all of them sniffling and coughing and dying from the fever or the cold itself. There was so much she didn't know about Indiana and this trip. Lucy was scared. She wanted to stay.

Nicey knocked and entered the cabin with the kids, hers and Lucy's. When she saw the look on her friend's face, she directed her children to wait outside. Then she sat down with Lucy, and for a long moment, they were silent. Lucy's bigger kids crawled into their beds, and the toddler hung from his mama's leg. Finally, Nicey spoke.

"He ain't in there no more," she said.

Lucy realized Nicey was talking about Frederick, and she

thought about how if they stayed, she wouldn't have to worry about him disappearing into Juda's cabin anymore. Everyone knew about the baby, but no one knew whose it was for sure. Juda wasn't exactly the saint of Spring Hill Plantation. Some folks think it could be Caleb's, and others say it was Master Rubin's. Some outright said it was Frederick's. No one knew. Lucy just wanted it all to be over.

Frederick opened the door and stood in the doorway. Nicey, seeing the wary look on Lucy's face when she saw Frederick, turned around to face him. "We going, Lucy," he said. "We will start preparing tomorrow." Then he pulled the door closed and left his wife to her company.

Frederick's family gathered around the table in Master Warwick's dining room. Dr. Patteson stood before them and spoke in an even tone. "As part of settling this estate, this house needs to be cleared out, and Master Warwick wanted all of you to have the first choice of his belongings to take for your new home." The family stared at the man in disbelief. "Before you start, just know that I already bought some extra blankets to supplement the house stock so that everyone will have a warm bedroll," he said and pointed to the stacks against the far wall. Lucy headed for the piles of linens and blankets and began rolling them up to divide among the families.

"Lucy," Dr. Patteson said, "you can leave that for the moment. I think Master Warwick would want you to partake in the gift of his belongings first, before I open the house up to the rest of the folks." Lucy nodded. Then he turned to Frederick and put his hand on the man's shoulder. "This is what John wanted for you as his son."

Frederick nodded and looked down at the large polished oak table. It was true, he thought. All of those years that he drove John

Warwick around town, tended to his horses and his guests, and even tended to Warwick as he got older, and he didn't know the man was his father. Part of Frederick didn't want to believe it. But another part of him thought he always had an idea about that. Frederick ran his hand across the top of the large, polished oak table. He'd been thinking about starting a school once they got settled, and this table could accommodate sixteen people. The chairs were high backs with woven straw seats, and a tall cabinet stood in the corner. This furniture would be perfect for his school, and he imagined that Warwick already knew that.

Frederick said, "I want as many books as possible from the library."

"Books?" asked Dr. Patteson.

"I want to start a school," Frederick said.

"Of course, you do," Dr. Patteson said and smiled. He went over the specifics of what would and would not be reasonable for the trip in the wagons. Then he walked out into the grand entryway, and the family followed. "We have a very short time allocated, Frederick, so let me know as soon as your family has finished collecting their items."

Frederick nodded and directed his boys to start loading the dining room table and chairs.

Martha hesitated at the door of the library as if waiting for Master Warwick to wave her in. He usually stood leaning against the fireplace mantle. In spite of his becoming lame at the end, and seemingly weak, he always looked exactly right standing in his library.

"It's okay, Martha," a voice whispered, and she jumped, her eyes darting around the room for her former master. "You can go in." A chill ran through her, and she shivered. Frederick Jr. gently nudged her from behind. "You allowed," he said, and Martha sighed.

Martha headed straight for the Norton astronomy book. Master Warwick had moved this book to the bottom shelf the day they talked about Aquila the Eagle. Eagles were free to soar atop the trees, and they could see exactly what was coming from a distance. Martha wanted that kind of ability. He'd let her read from it many times after his guests had left. As Frederick Jr. rummaged around the fireplace mantle and through the man's desk, Martha slid the book from its place and sat on the floor, legs crossed with the book in her lap. She unfolded a large illustration of the planets and ran her fingers around the edge of the sun, which took up most of the diagram. She closed her eyes and promised that she would learn the names of all the planets and stars, and then she would teach them to the children. *Just as you told me.* When she folded the illustration back up, she noticed writing on the inside cover of the book: *From the Library of John Warwick*, and a tear fell onto the page.

"Ay, yes," Frederick Jr. said as he reached into the back of one of the desk drawers and pulled out two slender leather cases. He sat down on the floor next to Martha and studied the sheaths. One was engraved with an ox and the other with an eagle in flight. Then he pulled a long, fixed-blade knife from its case and held it up. "Look at that." It shined like nothing he'd ever seen. He slid it back into the sheath, slid it into his boot, and then he nodded a smile as if this knife had been forged for him all along. The eagle sheath was decorated with tassels sliced from the softest of leather. He handed it to Martha and nodded for her to look at it. She did. This knife also shined as if it were never used. When she slid it back into the sheath, she ran her finger along the wings of the eagle.

"Here," Frederick Jr. said. He grabbed it and slid it into her boot. "We don't know what's out there. You should have this to protect yourself." Slightly shorter than his, it was the perfect size for her. "Keep it out of sight. We're not allowed weapons."

In the parlor, Lucy wandered about in a daze. "Anything in the house," Lucy repeated to herself as if repeating it would help her to believe it. Yellowed lace hung from rods over the floor-length windows, and dust had settled into the huge floral rug centered in the room. Master Warwick never used this room. Everything was exactly as the missus had left it. Lucy slipped off her shoes and closed her eyes as her hardened feet nestled into the softness of the carpet. Never having had this privilege, her soles ached for relief. Still, there was no room in the wagons for comforts as such. "Necessities not niceties," Patteson had warned. "Anything in the house—pssh," she mumbled and slipped on her shoes again.

The wagon train included sixteen wagons. Eight covered for families, two cook wagons, and six for supplies, animals, equipment, and household goods. Dr. Patteson's buggy was the seventeenth vehicle. Patteson hired a man to get the wagon train successfully to Indiana. Foard had made the trek several times before and was familiar with the terrain. He brought horses and taught the men how to shoot on horseback, how to carry a rifle safely, and how to hide it quickly. He had helped move freed slaves in the past, but it was usually a family or two in a couple of wagons. He'd never heard of an entire plantation of slaves being freed. Because of this, he hired a couple of scouts as well.

The family Conestoga wagons had six mattresses. They were six feet by two feet, and they covered the sloping floor. Dr. Patteson had purchased the modern cotton-stuffed mattresses that they would keep. Frederick's family was to share a wagon with Wilson's family of three, including slow Mary Elizabeth, or Mary E, as Martha liked to call her. Martha had plans to start teaching Mary E how to read during their travels.

Rubin had assigned the smaller families he thought could get along. The single men and women were also assigned.

Lucy stepped out onto the back porch, grinning. The men were busy loading the gigantic dining room table, and Nicey had just finished hanging pots and pans onto the side of the kitchen wagon.

"Where have you been?" Nicey said. Lucy sat down on the porch step and waved for her friend to join her. Nicey moaned as she sat and then turned to Lucy. "You got some kind of sneakiness going on there. What is with you?" Lucy laughed and pulled a decorative glass perfume bottle from her pocket. "Oh my," Nicey said. "You have been in that woman's room." Lucy looked thoughtfully at the bottle. It was true. She'd gone up to Mrs. Warwick's room. Just like the parlor, it was untouched, as if the woman were there that morning, with the exception of several layers of dust. Even though Patteson did say "anything in the house," slipping the bottle into her pocket felt like stealing from a dead woman. Nicey leaned over to sniff the rim of the bottle, and Lucy laughed.

"Here," Lucy said and put the bottle in her hand.

"What you say?"

"Take it. I ain't got no use for it," Lucy said as she stood up from the step. Then she nodded toward Juda, waddling away from the wagons. "I ain't doing that no more." The ladies laughed, and Nicey waved her off. She sprayed the air, sniffed, and dropped the bottle quickly into her pocket.

Patrick was to share a wagon with Pleasant's family, much to Martha's disappointment.

"I can't believe that I'm free. I can't wait to settle in Indiana," said Patrick.

"We are all free," said Pleasant, helping Patrick load.

Frederick lifted a bundle for Frederick Jr. to load into the wagon, and Frederick Jr. made a face. "Books?" He shook his head. "All the nice things in that house, and you want books?"

Frederick shrugged. "Cover them good," he added.

On the front porch, Patteson supervised the distribution of linens and bedding among all the other families. To prepare for the cold, he'd bought ponchos and hats for the men and hooded ponchos for the women. These would also serve as extra blankets. Even the young girls were given long pants, and later, they gladly tossed their tattered, dirty shirtdresses into the bonfire.

Lucy was packing some plates and bowls into a crate. As Wesley waited to carry it out to the wagon, she noticed she had some room left. "Watch this for a minute," she said, and then she disappeared. When she returned, she was wrapping two fancy Haviland dinner bowls in a dish towel. She slid them into the crate and nodded to Wesley to take them away.

When the big house was opened up to the rest of the families, it was chaos. Pictures were ripped off the walls, and children jumped on the beds. Patrick found the Warwick coat of arms that featured Warwick holding a shield. Annise wanted some nice shoes she'd heard about, but they were already gone, so she settled for a satiny robe from Mrs. Warwick's wardrobe.

By late afternoon, Patteson had to cut off the scavenging so that pens could be built for the chickens and tethers wrapped to keep the goats moving beside the wagons. There was too much to do before first light. Patteson had Martha run through the house and clear the rooms of people, and just before they walked out the front door, she heard something, causing her to stop.

"What?" Patteson said. His voice echoed through the emptied rooms. He was holding the door open, waiting. Martha looked around. Curtain rods had been pulled down, and dark ovals and rectangles decorated the walls where pictures had once hung. While she couldn't figure out where the noise came from, something didn't feel right. The silence was eerie.

"Oh, nothing," she said, and then she stepped out onto the front porch. Dr. Patteson sighed and locked the door.

In the lane in front of the plantation, the wagons were moved into a circle, and a bonfire was started as the sun began to set. With everything packed for departure the next day, the families would start their bedroll practice that night, sleeping in either their wagons, in the hay in the barn, or on the floors of their cabins for one last time. "Get some rest tonight," Patteson yelled out from the center of the circle. He too would be sleeping in his buggy this night. "We roll at sunrise."

In the cabin, Frederick Jr. spread hay on the floor. Martha sat looking down from the loft, her legs swinging in the air, and her sister tucked in, humming nearby. "Stop that damn humming," Wesley laughed. "No one is going to be sleeping tonight." They all looked at Lucy sitting on the floor against the wall, and their baby brother curled up, sleeping next to her. "Except for him," he added, and the boys chuckled.

Lucy sat stone-faced. She didn't address her children at all when they came in, and she hadn't spoken since. They all noticed it. Awhile later, Frederick entered, and Lucy stood up and wiped some hay from her dress. Martha stopped swinging her legs, and the boys settled down. Suddenly, the air was different in the cabin, and Martha was holding her breath. Frederick stepped toward his wife, but Lucy walked out the door. Martha huffed, climbed down from the loft, and walked out too.

A few men sat around the fire. One poked at it with a stick and shook his head. Martha could hear the low mumble of their talking from the roof of the kitchen house. She stared up into the stars and tried to imagine what it would be like to be free. She pictured herself teaching kids to read and write at one end of the big dining room table that the boys loaded for her daddy's school. She tried to imagine herself with a husband and a cabin of her own, but Patrick's face appeared, sitting next to Pleasant, who was reading to him, and Martha pounded the roof. What does freedom even look like?

Suddenly, Martha heard something behind the kitchen house.

She rolled over and peeked over the edge toward the big house, but she saw nothing.

The next morning, everyone was in or near their assigned wagons as the sun peeked on the eastern horizon. It promised to be a bright, sunny day. Several people had been taught how to harness, drive, and care for the mules, which were hitched and ready to move. No one slept well the night before, and all were up early, meandering around their respective wagons. Even the mules were becoming restless. "I thought we started at sunrise," someone shouted, and mumbling traveled down the line. One of the scouts on horseback circled the train for a count. Everyone watched as Dr. Patteson climbed into his buggy and got comfortable on the leather seats behind Frederick, his driver. The top was down, and he turned back toward the train.

"Wagons, roll!"

Drivers slapped the reins on the backs of their mules and yelled, "Yah."

Pans hung from the sides of the wagons sounded like broken calliopes generating random, competing notes. They were on the half-mile-long drive to the main road. The women began a song, and soon, everyone joined the chorus. This was the beginning of a celebration of freedom.

Before the train turned onto the main road, someone yelled "fire," and a commotion started. Some jumped off their wagons, and the train came to a stop. The big house was engulfed in flames. Some of the folks moved as if to save it, but Foard placed his scouts in the way to stop them.

"Nothing we can do now," shouted Foard. "It's too late."

They watched the fire as it spread to the cabins. Lucy, who had all but grown up on this plantation, pounded the side of the wagon. The disrespect of a decent man made her beyond angry.

Dr. Patteson, still in his buggy, shook his head. Then he held his hand up in the air, and Foard yelled, "Wagons, roll!"

As the wagons turned west on the main road, the people, many with tears in their eyes, took a last look as the big house caved in. Black smoke rose from the area of their cabins.

Martha, walking along the side of the wagon, began to sing, "*O Mamma, O Mamma. Place Congo is calling, O Mamma, O Mamma. Place Congo is calling for the Congo dance, O Mamma, O Mamma.*"

With less enthusiasm, others joined the singing that now felt like a funeral dirge.

"This song makes me think of free people in Africa," said Frederick Jr., who was driving their mules.

"It helps me keep movin'," Martha said.

Patteson was heartbroken. "How could that fire get started?"

Shaking his head, Frederick said, "It had help. It wasn't God's will."

A man who lived along the main road came out onto his porch to watch the exodus. Seeing the group, he spat off to the side. "Good riddance."

Part II

The Long Road to Freedom
What dangers will they face?

. . . it shall not be lawfull for any negroe or other slave to carry or arme himselfe with any club, staffe, gunn, sword or any other weapon of defence or offence . . .

Virginia Law (1680)

November 1848, On The Road

Chapter 7 Friends and Neighbors?

The morning sun shined through the oaks and pines, lighting up the first layers of fallen leaves on the ground. Many of the people had already moved several times in an effort to sit comfortably in the wagon before they finally gave up and walked alongside. They had passed three farmhouses already. These weren't plantations by any means. Barely enough vegetables were growing in weedy gardens to feed a family. Martha guessed that the men who lived there probably hunted their food, or they knew some kind of trade like metal-making. She'd have to look up the correct name for that later from Frederick's stash of encyclopedias.

Beside one house, a young woman wearing a housedress more raggedy than any dress that Martha herself wore, was hanging dingy clothes on a rope tied between two trees. Martha realized then that the finer dresses she and her family wore were intended for going into town and on special occasions at the big house, gifts from Master Warwick. This girl, who worked in her dresses, didn't seem surprised at all to see the caravan. She pulled a pair of wet britches from her basket, and when she stood up, she noticed Martha. They locked eyes. The girl was her age, and Martha suddenly felt they had some kind of commonality, a comradery even, as if they could have been friends if she weren't moving away from the Lynchburg area. Martha waved to the girl, a small wave before she looked back to the ground ahead of her. It felt like a secret wave. When she looked back, the girl raised her chin up in the air and spat on the ground in Martha's direction. Then she grabbed the basket and disappeared into her farmhouse.

Nicey started singing again in a kindhearted attempt to distract them from their woes.

"O Mamma, O Mamma. The Congo priest is rattling his cha-cha! O Mamma, O Mamma. The Congo priest is rattling for the Congo dance! O Mamma, O Mamma . . ."

By midafternoon, Foard halted the train next to a field on the western side of the trail. On the other side was a shallow stream. During the short stop, the mules were given water and allowed to graze. Riders traded spots with walkers, and the smaller children who had grown restless played chase in the nearby grass. Martha climbed into the wagon, leaned against the sideboard, and took a deep breath. A few moments to close her eyes would be fine, she thought.

She listened to the muffled sounds of people talking and stretch-moaning, their normally active muscles clenched from sitting most of the day. The tone of their conversations seemed upbeat and inquisitive. No one complained. And in the distance, the screaming laughter of children. Martha knew the sound. They sounded like schoolchildren. White ones.

Suddenly, gunshots rang out, and the women screamed. Children were corralled quickly back into their wagons, and everyone ducked as low as they could. The scouts had their guns at the ready. Then an old man had appeared at the front of the caravan on horseback.

"This is my land!" the old man said to Dr. Patteson. He sat on his horse, the butt of his rifle on his thigh, ready to shoot again if needed, but next time, it might not be a warning shot. "You all need to move along."

Foard got the wagons moving again, and as they crawled forward, he suddenly directed the horsemen to change positions. One of the scouts called out "Left!" and the freed horsemen moved to the left side of the covered wagons. The scouts were to watch over the right side. This was new to the men, but when they pulled far enough ahead, they understood why. On the right side of the trail, a dozen slaves leaned over rows of cotton. The old horseman had rejoined them, and when one of his slaves tried to glance over at the wagon train, he let loose a warning shot over their heads. This caravan of newly freed slaves was to be none of their business.

They continued down the trail, the pace slowing as the afternoon progressed. They passed brown cotton rows, hayfields, and an apple orchard. They were amazed by the sights of large plantation homes with grand brick entrances leading to sprawling green lawns, stately mansions that made Master Warwick's house seem plain. As the sun moved into the western sky, they passed a small farmhouse with children playing in the dirt out front and their mama slamming windows on the first floor as a crisp wind had picked up moments before. When the woman saw Patrick riding on horseback, she gasped and froze. Then she yelled out something, and a man appeared on the front porch holding a rifle. He called his children into the house. One of the scouts followed behind Patrick and tipped his hat to the man who then sat down in a rocking chair, rifle across his lap. Suddenly, it seemed that everyone was as tired as the mules.

As the sun reached the horizon on the trail and the sky filled with color, Foard yelled, "Circle wagons!"

Dr. Patteson's carriage, while not large, had springs, a top that went up and down, and was way more comfortable than the wagons. Foard took charge of Dr. Patteson's buggy and pulled it into place to create the circle.

Everyone worked as a team to set up camp. The men tended to the corralling and feeding of the mules, goats, and other animals while the boys gathered firewood. Several of the older girls kept the small children occupied, and the women prepared beds for their families and helped with the cooking. Martha and Mary E took buckets toward the tree line to fetch water from a stream that one of the scouts had tracked before they stopped.

Lucy and Nicey were in charge of the cook wagons, covered wagons with side and rear flaps. Once they stopped, Nicey pulled up the rear flap where a board dropped down and formed a table with a post under it holding it in place. She retrieved a smoked ham, and one of her children carried some onions to the board table to be chopped.

The two covered supply wagons were loaded with several fifty-pound sacks of flour and cornmeal, smoked meats, dried fruit, jars of jams, and beans. They could only carry two thousand pounds; otherwise, the wheels might break. No one was to ride in these wagons for the maximum weight limit and because, well, they couldn't afford for any food to disappear.

Martha and Mary E. followed Patrick and Frederick Jr., who were leading four horses toward the tree line until Patrick directed them upstream a bit as they were to collect clean water for drinking and cooking. Once they found the stream through all the trees, Martha reached her hand into the cool water and patted the back of her neck. She wet a corner of her dress and used it to wipe the day's grime from her face. Then she tilted her bucket in the water and watched it slowly fill. Young Mary E had sat down on a tall root and was taking her shoes off.

"What are you doing?"

"This water look nice, don't it, Miss Martha?" Mary E stood up and grabbed her bucket.

"Are you crazy? That water is colder than you know."

That didn't stop Mary E. She jumped with both feet into the stream and let out a squeal. Then she raised her chin like it was nothing and moved to the middle. Leaning over, she filled her bucket quickly from there.

"Look, Miss Martha, my bucket is already full."

Martha shook her head. "You got a bucket of mud is what you got." Mary E looked down at the brown mess and tried to lift it to dump it, but it was too heavy for her little arms. Martha laughed. "Kick it over with your foot." The girl kicked it until it toppled over, then she laughed. "Now, don't step in front of your bucket, Mary E. That brings up the bottom." Martha showed her how to tilt the bucket only slightly and keep an eye on the water so that leaves and bugs didn't drift in.

When Martha's bucket was full, and Mary E's was half full, Martha placed their buckets on the bank of the stream.

"Get your shoes, Mary E," she said.

Before the girl could finish with her shoes, a tall man in a cowboy hat grabbed both of the girls by the elbows. Mary E screamed, and Martha twisted her arm in all different directions, but his grip was hard and strong. Mary E stopped wiggling and cried, pee running down her leg.

"Boss," he said. An older man had appeared on the other side of the stream. "What you want me to do with them?"

"Well, these two came from somewhere. We need to find out where."

Just then, Foard calmly said, "Stop now." His rifle was raised and aimed at the man across the stream. When he moved to reach for his gun, Foard said, "Don't. We ain't here to cause no trouble. Our man is coming."

Patrick had ridden off to fetch help, and he was already on the way back with Dr. Patteson on horseback in the lead. Patteson, with one hand in the air, holding the reins with the other, was repeatedly yelling, "Hold up now! Hold up!" When they reached the group, both men dismounted and stepped forward. In the meantime, Foard was sizing up the older man and his ranch hand.

Patteson spoke, "We don't intend to cause any trouble, sir."

The older man shifted his weight to the other foot, seemingly relaxed that two white men were in charge. He crossed the stream to talk to Patteson face-to-face. Then he nodded to his man, who let the girls go. As Patrick led the girls out of the trees and back to camp, the ranch hand stepped out to watch them.

The ranch hand returned to the group. "Boss, they got more than a dozen wagons circled in the east field."

The old man glared at the doctor. "How many colored you got on my land?"

Patteson explained about the number of families, that their manumission papers were on hand, so it wasn't an abetting situation, and that they could be gone as early as first light.

The old man seemed a little stumped, either by Patteson's approach or simply by the fact that he'd never heard of so many freed slaves in one place, not to mention seeing colored men riding horses.

Patteson pulled several neatly folded banknotes from his jacket pocket and held them up in front of the man. "Would this help for the night's use of your land on this quiet and beautiful evening?"

The man smiled. He took the notes, placed them quickly into his pocket, and nodded to his new friends before heading back across the stream.

The sky darkened, and folks slowly trickled in from their chores. With the mules tended to and the animals grazing in quickly rigged pens of branches tied to trees, all but a few men lined up to the cook fire with a cup in hand. Caleb nodded to Nicey as she ladled soup into his cup. In it was a chunk of ham, which felt like a treat after this first day of travel. He ate leaning against a wagon. He knew if he sat down, he would need help getting up.

Everyone gathered around campfires. The slurping turned from soup to sauce as solemn faces stared into the glowing embers.

"What a day," Bil-Buck said as he sat down at the fire where other young adults had gathered. Patrick stared into the flames. Frederick Jr. was leaning over a stick, digging a hole. Martha was reading a book by firelight. "I know we on our way to freedom, but this a long day."

"Ain't going to be free," Patrick said, not taking his eyes off the fire.

"What you mean? We moving, ain't we?" Bil-Buck said.

Patrick glared at Bil-Buck. "Didn't you see the big house burning?"

Martha glanced up from her book. She knew this tone, this side of Patrick, and that he was only getting started.

"Did you not hear the white man shooting at us?" Patrick continued, flinging a twig into the fire.

Bil-Buck nodded. "Sure, Patrick, I did." Then he looked around at the rest of the faces. "I don't know about the house, but the other was one man, and both of them's behind us."

"There'll be more!" Patrick said and flung a larger stick into the fire. Sparks flew into the air above and carried close to their faces. Pleasant, not used to Patrick's outbursts, offered sweetly to read to him. He stood up and brushed off his pants. "No, I don't want you to read to me."

Martha stifled a laugh and turned a page in her book.

Patrick moved to Bil-Buck and looked down at him. "You didn't see it."

"I heard the shots . . ."

"No. You didn't see the man who grabbed Martha and Mary Elizabeth," Patrick said and sneered.

"Grab Martha?" Bil-Buck said. He looked at her.

"You didn't watch them wiggle and squirm while he held them in place like they were his pigs."

Martha stared back into her book, wishing Patrick wouldn't take things so far.

"Next bastard that aims a gun at me," Patrick added, pointing at his chest, "I'm going to shoot him."

Martha looked up at him, then at Bil-Buck, who had inched closer to her.

"Are you okay?" he said.

Frederick Jr. spoke, not looking up from his poking hole. "They didn't want no trouble." Patrick huffed and paced. "No coloreds can be on white man's land," Frederick Jr. continued and looked up at Patrick. "They needed to make sure we wasn't runaways."

"So you say," Patrick added.

"We still here, ain't we?" Frederick Jr. turned back to poking at his hole. "They just needed to . . . what you say . . . check us out."

"I'm fine," Martha said to Bil-Buck, then turned back to her book.

"There will be more. There will always be a white man ready to shoot," Patrick said.

"That's true," Frederick Jr. said. "We are more responsible for ourselves and each other than ever before."

"All I know is we going that way," Bil-Buck said and pointed in the direction of the road. Martha looked up at the North Star, realized Bil-Buck was pointing westward, and she smiled at him. He continued, "They is so much ahead of us. It's like a new world is opening up."

"New world!" Martha said. She elbowed Bil-Buck and said, "Listen here." Then she read aloud from the page she was just reading in her book.

"I have often been asked how I felt when first I found myself on free soil. And my readers may share the same curiosity. There is scarcely anything in my experience about which I could not give a more satisfactory answer. A new world had opened upon me."

She grinned at Bil-Buck and then continued reading.

"If life is more than breath, and the 'quick round of blood,' I lived more in one day than in a year of my slave life. It was a time of joyous excitement which words can but tamely describe. In a letter written to a friend soon after reaching New York, I said: 'I felt as one might feel upon escape from a den of hungry lions.' Anguish and grief, like darkness and rain, may be depicted; but gladness and joy, like the rainbow, defy the skill of pen or pencil."

Bil-Buck asked what she was reading.

Martha said, "This is Frederick Douglass's story of his life."

"I think I like Frederick Douglass. And I like how you read it, Martha," Bil-Buck said.

Martha saw the reflection of firelight dancing in his eyes. She could feel that this man was speaking the truth, and she wanted to continue reading to him, but she knew her limits. Glancing around the group, she noticed Pleasant frowning at the book in her own lap, *Mary Had a Little Lamb*, and Martha couldn't help but smile. Turning back to Bil-Buck, his eyes were still on her like bees on honey. Perhaps he'd like for her to read to him again the following night? Martha was pretty sure she didn't need to offer.

"I'm interested in the fact that the less secure a man is, the more likely he is to have extreme prejudice."

- Clint Eastwood

Winter, 1848, At New Virginia Turnpike

Chapter 8
The Toll Booth

A toll booth came into view up ahead, and Foard yelled out, "Wagons, whoa." The Virginia Turnpike was a fairly new roadway built of boards. It ran from Staunton, Virginia, to Kenova, Virginia, where passengers could take a ferry across the Ohio River. They were entering the turnpike just outside of Lexington. Foard warned that their trip across the Shenandoah Valley had gone well, but they still had a long way to go. "And those tall mountains on the horizon," he pointed into the distance, "promise to be our biggest challenge." At least, this new road was going to make for a much-smoother ride.

The gate was a long, trimmed tree that was lifted by moving a heavy stone tied to the thick end of the tree. Two smaller logs formed an X fulcrum that allowed the tree to be raised or lowered. Fencing and deep ditches blocked any attempt to avoid the gate. A uniformed man emerged from a new gatehouse. As they approached, Patteson took a sheet of banknotes. His buggy stopped in front of an astonished man.

"What is this all about?" asked the toll collector.

"I'm Dr. Patteson, and I have seventy-five colored and four white men, including me. We are rolling sixteen wagons pulled by thirty-eight mules. A small herd of sheep and some goats follow the wagons," said Patteson, climbing down from the buggy.

"Where you headed?"

"Indiana."

"Those must be free slaves. I ain't never seed so many folks and wagons befo'. I ain't sure how much to charge you."

"What do you usually charge?"

"Fifty cents fer a person and same fer a wagon or animals."

"Well, then, I think fifty dollars would cover the whole wagon train and three for your trouble," said Patteson handing the man the banknotes.

"Dis is mo' than I gits in a good summer month when wagons with stuff to sell are headed west to the Ohio River."

"Thank you, sir. Now, if you will raise the gate, we will be on our way," said Patteson climbing into the buggy.

The man raised the gate, and Frederick urged the buggy forward.

The toll collector, still shaking his head and watching while the buggy passed, shouted, "Oh, I almost forgot. Dey be waitin' for you somewhere's along dis pike."

The ride became smoother than the rutted, bumpy dirt and stone roads they had just left. Lunch was eaten with the wagons rolling.

Sam, the forward scout, rode rapidly toward them, waving his hands. Foard shouted, "Wagons, whoa."

Many armed men were blocking the road ahead. After a brief conference, Patteson mounted a horse, and the four white men formed a line holding rifles across their saddles. Frederick closely followed the riders, and another rifle barrel was visible. Patrick's wagon, with a barrel showing, pulled beside the buggy. They were stopped when a rider in the center of eight riders held up his hand. At the apparent leader's signal, the confronting riders holstered their rifles, and Patteson signaled his men to holster their rifles.

Two men from the middle of the band of horses urged their horses forward toward the line. The one wearing a badge said, "I'm Sheriff Baxter from Covington. What's goin' on?"

Patteson and the sheriff were sizing up each other. Baxter was short and stout, and Patteson was a head taller and had broader shoulders. Baxter loosened the strap above his pistol. Foard's rifle, while holstered, could be rotated and fired quickly. No one wanted to fire the first shot.

Dr. Patteson broke the silence. "I'm Dr. Patteson. I'm in charge of this wagon train on our way to a free state. What right do you have to stop us?"

Baxter had to look up to talk to Dr. Patteson, and he said, "I'm the sheriff in these parts. I can stop anybody, anywhere, anytime I want. I ain't never seen so many colored. Y'all ain't plannin' a revolt."

"Oh, God no," said Patteson, laughing. "A wealthy Quaker gave them their freedom from Amherst County upon his death, and I have a copy of his will naming each of them. I have their manumission papers. As you know, Sheriff, they have to leave Virginia."

"How many free slaves are in all dem wagons?"

"There are seventy-five colored, counting two babies. We need to make camp before nightfall and build fires," said Patteson.

Baxter looked at the rifle barrels still aimed at the posse from the buggy and one wagon. The long-bearded man nodded slightly. He said, squinting, "I cain't reed, but shouldn't you check dem papers?"

Patteson, holding up a copy of the Patrick for Sheriff Baxter, said, "You can readily see they are all freed by name in this document."

"I don't want no trouble from y'all," said Baxter, waving his men to the side of the road.

Patteson quickly folded the probated will and slid it back in his inside coat pocket. The sheriff's posse moved to one side of the road.

Foard and the scouts moved to the other side of the road.

"Wagons, roll," had never been heard more clearly.

Patteson joined Foard and the scouts. His buggy and driver were the first to pass the eight men, and the other wagons followed closely. Patrick slowly turned his wagon and joined the row of wagons at the rear. After everyone passed, Patteson said, "Good day, Sheriff. We have some miles to make up."

Six of the men followed the sheriff east on the turnpike. Two men, who Patteson thought looked like Al and Bill, left the pike for the woods.

The wagons rolled until the sun was low on the horizon. Foard announced as people gathered around the cooks' fire, "We want you all to know that there may be some danger lingering in the woods."

"Is it wolves?" asked Martha.

Smiling, Foard said, "No. Something more dangerous. Two men, whom you probably know, are following our wagons. They would like to catch one or more of you who might stray from the wagons. Starting tonight, I want an armed man with people gathering firewood and children fetching water. Anyone stopping in the bushes while we are rolling must have a guard."

The people built fires inside and outside the circle. The guards on duty kept them fueled, and there were six in each shift. Foard was making sure no one would come near the wagons.

Patteson rode over to Frederick's wagon. "Frederick, your campfire stories might help folks relax tonight."

Frederick said, "I have just the thing for tonight." The people needed no orders on this.

It was a chilly night, and a large group gathered around one of the cooking fires. Frederick stood before them. "I want to read you some definitions of words from some newspaper clippings Master Warwick saved."

Groans and moans emanated from all around the circle. "Hush, now," said Frederick with a grin. "Let me tell you about Ambrose Bierce. Bierce was born at Horse Cave Creek in Meigs County, Ohio."

Shaking his head, Frederick Jr. said, "Horse Cave Creek? Well, what is it? A horse or a cave or a creek?"

Some laughter erupted, then Frederick continued. "His parents were poor, but well read. They instilled in him a deep love for books and writing. That's what Martha and I are trying to instill in all of you."

"If Martha's teachin', I'm in," said Bil-Buck as he winked at her.

"Ambrose grew up in Indiana, the state where we are headed. He attended high school. He was the tenth of thirteen children whose father gave all of them names beginning with the letter A. In order of birth, Ambrose's brothers and sisters were—Abigail, Amelia, Ann, Addison, Aurelius, Augustus, Almeda, Andrew, Albert, Ambrose, Arthur, Adelia, and Aurelia."

Everyone laughed, and Lucy said, "Maybe I will rename all of my children with the letter Z. That would be good."

Martha laughed. "Are there even eight names that begin with Z?"

Amid more laughter, Frederick continued, "Ambrose left home at age fifteen to become a printer's devil at a small Ohio newspaper."

Lucy said with one eyebrow up, "Doesn't sound like the right side of the Bible to me."

"It's not like the devil I preach about. This devil works for a printer doing mostly dirty work, odd jobs, and some writing," said Frederick. "I want to read to you a few of the definitions he wrote. Here is one of my favorites: 'Lawyer, one skilled in circumvention of the law.'"

Amid chuckles and snorts, Patteson said, "That's why I became a doctor."

"Let me see," said Frederick, flipping through some clippings. "Aw, yes, 'Doctor, a man who confirms that you are sick and will be well in a few days in exchange for your money.'"

"My favorite: 'Bride, a woman who willingly forgoes the future prospect of happiness,'" said Frederick, looking at Lucy.

Several of the women nodded and said, "Amen."

"How about some music?" said Patteson.

Curtis, one of the scouts, pulled a banjo from his wagon and began playing some lively tunes. Wesley watched intensely. Then he moved to sit beside him and studied the movement of his fingers.

"Could I try to play your banjo?" Wesley asked.

"Well, yes, but just a few strokes. You know it takes a long time to learn how to play one of these things," Curtis said, handing the banjo to Wesley.

Wesley strummed and picked as if he were warming up, then started playing the last song that Curtis had played.

Patteson asked, "Where did you learn that?"

"I don't know, just watchin' and listenin', I guess," said Wesley handing the banjo back to the scout.

Curtis played another song and handed the banjo back to Wesley. With little difficulty, Wesley strummed the tune.

Curtis shook his head and said, "I've only heard about people who can do what you just did. I never believed it 'til now. Wait here. I have an older banjo that's missing a wire. You would be welcome to have it."

Patteson said, "Well, Wesley, from now on, you will have the

THE PRICE OF FREEDOM IN 1848, title, 'Banjo Boy.'"

Foard approached Patteson with some news, and the concern on his face bit into the laughter of the crowd. Patteson nodded at him.

Foard yelled out, "All right, everyone. Tonight, we need all of you inside your wagons for the duration of the night. It's going to be an early morning." The men were directed to fuel the fires to provide as much heat and light as possible and to get their families inside. For the rest of the night, Foard and his men kept a tight patrol.

The next morning, there would be no time for a hot breakfast. They ate hardtack and drank coffee. Foard, looking rough with bags under his eyes, yelled, "Wagons, roll." As the caravan got moving, the sun peaked over the mountain ridge behind them. For lunch, they stopped the wagons long enough to pass out some bread and smoked meat, but then they were moving again, eating as they walked. Finally, Foard circled the wagons just as the sun began to set.

After dinner, Martha gathered the older children into her wagon, where they sat on mattresses and prepared for their reading lessons by lighting candles. As she began to read the first sentences, a group of adults joined them, also wanting to learn. Martha found this helpful. The adults were easier to teach because they paid attention and helped keep the children in line. Martha wrote a word on the slate and asked one of the children to read it.

"In-dee-en."

"That's close," Martha said. Then one of the adults spoke up.

"Indiana," she said. "It's where we're going."

"That's right," said Martha.

A box of chalk taken from the master's desk would have to last until the long journey was over.

The McGuffey Reader was good for keeping their attention on letters and for learning a variety of words containing the letters. The illustrations also evoked many questions. "Did the cat eat the rat?" Martha wrote out the question and underlined the new word, "eat." The boys giggled, and the girls felt sorry for the rat.

"What was the fan for?" asked Charles from John and Kitty's family. He pointed to the small sailboat. At first, no one knew what it was. Then George, one of the adults in Nicey's family who had been hired out, said he had been to the docks, and he described the giant sailboats to everyone's amazement. Many had seen barges on the James River, but only one could describe a giant ship with great sheets propelling it across deep water. Kitty said her great-grandmother had been chained in the bottom of a great ship with many other captured people. "That's how our ancestors all came here. Those who survived," she said.

These stories kept everyone's attention, and Martha did the best she could to teach letters and words from the stories.

After the children went to their wagons, George asked if Martha would read more of Douglass's book. Bil-Buck smiled and nodded in agreement and hope. Martha handed him a candle to hold, and she read from Frederick Douglass's life story.

My mother and I were separated when I was but an infant—before I knew her as my mother. It is a common custom . . . For what this separation is done, I do not know, unless it be to hinder the development of the child's affection toward its mother, and to blunt and destroy the natural affection of the mother for the child. This is the inevitable result.

I never saw my mother, to know her as such, more than four or five times in my life; and each of these times was very short in duration, and at night. She was hired by a Mr. Stewart, who lived about twelve miles from my home. She made her journeys to see me in the night, travelling the whole distance on foot, after the performance of her day's work. She was a field hand, and a whipping is the penalty of not being in the field at sunrise, unless a slave has special permission from his or her master to the contrary—a permission which they seldom get, and one that gives to him that gives it the proud name of being a kind master. I do not recollect of ever seeing my mother by the light of day. She was with me in the night. She would lie down with me and get me to sleep, but long before I waked she was gone. Very little communication ever took place between us.

Martha closed the book, and there was silence, as if their kind master, John Warwick himself, were in the space with them, summoned by the words of Douglass.

From what I know of the effect of these holidays upon the slave, I believe them to be among the most effective means in the hands of the slaveholder in keeping down the spirit of insurrection.

Frederick Douglass

December 1848, Mountains of Virginia

Chapter 9
Let It Snow, Let It Snow, Let It Snow

In the morning, the wagon circle looked like a snow fort as men pulled dry logs from under a wagon to start a campfire. The mules tied nearby had spent the night complaining and shaking the snow from their backs. The people had never seen this much snow on the plantation. The children had repeatedly been jumping into the high drifts between the wagons before they whined about their cold, wet hands and feet.

Everything was slower this morning, but eventually, Foard gave orders to get the mules moving, his own horse dancing in a circle trying to stay warm. It was time to start another day of travel.

Trail-breaking horses led the caravan, their steps clearing a path for the wagon wheels. Patrick manned the first wagon, his mules lifting their hooves higher than usual.

It took awhile for the mules to warm up enough to get back to their normal speed. Then suddenly, the first wagon stopped with a jolt, and Patrick was thrown forward between the mules and into the snow. The mules hawed and pulled with no movement until giving up.

Under the wagon, a downed tree blocked the wheels. This wagon train was going nowhere until that tree was cleared. Patrick stood up and unhooked his animals from the tongue.

It took several men crawling on their hands and knees under the front of the wagon to scrape the snow from the log. Then they chopped large branches from the tree and used them for leverage to move the trunk so a rope could be tied on.

Then, to the amazement of everyone in view, Foard jumped onto the back of one of the mules and straddled both of them with a foot on each animal. He took the reins and rope in one hand and snapped his whip with the other. The mules struggled and then eventually moved forward enough to drag the log completely off the turnpike. When Foard finally jumped down from his balancing act, the witnesses clapped and hurrahed.

Patrick and his wagon were sent to the back of the train, where the snow would be packed and easier on his now weakened wheels. He waited by the wayside as each wagon passed.

Nicey, who kept track of the days by marking the side of her wagon, knew that it was Christmas morning. While she longed for the celebration and restful days that Master Warwick afforded his slaves during the holidays, she knew there would be no occasion this year. Even if she had the men hunt down a couple of turkeys, there wouldn't be time to roast them as Foard needed to keep the wagons moving. But when she headed toward the cooking fire to start breakfast, she noticed two plucked turkeys and a hog lined up between baskets of potatoes, fresh greens, and a smaller basket with niceties like yeast, confectionary sugar, and a sack of cranberries. In the middle of the wagon circle, folks started hooting and hollering over a pine tree that showed up during the night. Since Charleston wasn't far away, Patteson had sent Foard and the scouts out during the night for supplies for the occasion. Seems they'd be celebrating Christmas after all!

Nicey and Lucy worked fast to get the turkeys and ham on the spits over three big fires and prepare the rest of the fixings. By mid-day, Nicey was ringing the cook's bell, which sounded extra special since today, it wasn't about soup.

In line, Wesley eyed the basket of sweetbread. It wasn't often they got soft bread dusted with sugar. His mouth watered . . . until Frederick Jr. grabbed the last two pieces.

"No!" Wes yelled out. Frederick Jr. laughed. "You're going to share that, aren't you?" Wes said.

"Why should I share it with you?" Frederick Jr. started.

"Knock it off, boys," Lucy said. "There's plenty of bread." She pulled out a pan, dumped the rolls into the basket, broke them apart, and held the basket up to Wes.

Wesley grabbed one and said, "Thank you, Mama." She nodded, and Wes added, "Oh, these are nice and hot." Lucy tossed a second one onto his plate. The Warwick clan enjoyed the feast sitting around the fires until their bellies were full. Then they rested, appreciating the day off from travel.

After dinner, Curtis produced two mules loaded with sacks. He passed boxes out to the girls, and in them were colorful dresses made of smooth fabrics. For many of the girls, this was the first dress they ever had. For the boys, he set down one tub full of footballs, baseballs, a wooden bat, some card games, a sack of marbles, and a set of dominoes. The boys had seen footballs before and immediately started kicking one around. Curtis put Nicey's boy in charge of the tub and its inventory to make sure it got packed away each time, then he pulled out a box and carried it to Martha.

"Martha, Dr. Patteson wanted you to have these." In it were two new slates and two boxes of chalk. She cried and hugged Curtis. Then she found Dr. Patteson and hugged him too. Everyone clapped and shouted, "Merry Christmas!"

Music started up near one of the fires as Banjo Boy and a couple of friends played on a one-string violin, a saw board in the shape of the letter C, and some upside-down buckets. People joined in the singing.

Bil-Buck approached the Christmas tree with a burning branch and lit the candles, one by one. A chorus of women began singing. This was a magical day for everyone.

Mary had a baby
Yes, Lord
Mary had a baby
Yes, Lord
The people keep a-coming and the train done gone
What did she name him?
Yes, Lord
What did she name him?
The people keep a-coming and the train done gone
She name him King Jesus
Yes, Lord
Name him King Jesus
Yes, Lord
Name him King Jesus

Yes, Lord

Martha led Bil-Buck by his hand behind a wagon and handed him a package. He unwrapped it and discovered a red scarf.

“Is this for me?”

“Yup, do you like it?”

“Did you make it?”

“I did.”

“It is beautiful and ever more since you made it.”

She took the long scarf and threw it over his head. She pulled him toward her and kissed him. Startled, Bil-Buck drew back.

“Merry Christmas, Bil-Buck,” said Martha, and she started to kiss him again, but he ducked under her outstretched arms and ran back to the inside of the circle.

Prejudices, it is well known, are most difficult to eradicate from the heart whose soil has never been loosened or fertilized by education: they grow there, firm as weeds among stones.

Charlotte Brontë, Annise Eyre

January 1849, Highest Mountains in Virginia

Chapter 10
She'll Be Comin''Round the Mountain

They had barely started rolling when Foard held up a halting signal. Several men jumped down from their wagons and were mumbling about what might be happening. Had something happened to one of the wagons?

Foard rode his horse to the middle of the string of wagons and signaled for the people to come close. "We are about to experience one of the hardest parts of this trip. We have to get these wagons down a steep hill that lies just ahead of us. The mules can't manage the hill tethered to a wagon, so we have to lower the wagons by rope. The scouts and I will show you how it's done with the first wagon, and then a team of you will manage the ropes as we lower all the wagons. We will need guards up and down. Those two are still around. If a posse comes, fire a warning shot."

The mules were unhitched, and Frederick Jr. was given the chore of leading theirs down the hill to the bottom. A camp was to be started at the bottom, and one of the cook wagons would go down early.

Foard tied a rope to the left side of Frederick's axle while Sam tied a rope to the right side. Both men walked their rope to a nearby pole that had been planted in the ground. The poles were planted to prevent the live trees from being girded and killed. Some men nodded to each other. They had been guessing about the use of the heavy ropes tied to one of the supply wagons.

"Unload anything you can carry down the hill," shouted Foard. "Women and children will also have to carry stuff. Pick anything you can manage and walk behind your wagon. Roll the table down on a pair of logs. We have to lighten the load in order to control the wagons."

"What about Frederick's books and my dishes?" asked Lucy.

"You are almost out of hands, so be selective and leave the rest on the side of the road. I knew this would happen, but I didn't want to argue with you at the plantation," said Foard.

Lucy carefully packed selected bowls in a sack that she could manage over her shoulder. Bil-Buck suggested that Martha make a sled out of one of the boxes. Then place as many books as she could manage on a sled that would slide down the road in front of her.

"What will happen to the other books?" Frederick asked.

"Maybe others will pick some up for you," said Bil-Buck. "I'll pass it down the line."

"But we won't know if anyone will," said Martha.

"No doubt, we will lose a few books like your mother lost some dishes," said Bil-Buck.

Frederick volunteered to carry a block for his wagon, and Wesley carried the other. These would be wedged in the front wheels whenever the wagon stopped. After the ropes were in place and ready for a slow release, the blocks would be pulled. The wagon started rolling slowly with Curtis guiding it by carrying the yoke. Their mules and horses followed them and enjoyed foraging while ropes were being moved.

They were surprised by how slowly the wagon crept and how tight the turns in the road were. Without the mules, the turns could be taken very sharply. The ropes were moved at every turn, even if they had only gone a short distance since the last move.

Curtis suddenly slipped and fell, and Frederick froze, then quickly recovered and blocked the wheel. Wesley did the same on his side of the wagon, and Frederick went to help Curtis. The men on the ropes had also tightened their hold by looping the ropes over, forming a loose but effective knot on the post.

Curtis had to be helped up but swore and fell when he tried to walk. Lucy put down her bag of dishes and helped him remove a boot. He tried but couldn't help cursing. She made a leg brace for him, and Frederick Jr. helped him onto his horse. He would ride back up and send someone down to guide the wagon.

After they started again, Martha was walking several yards behind her family group. Her load of books slowed her down. A strange man on horseback trotted from the woods. Before she could duck, he bent down and grabbed her around her midsection. He forced her facedown in front of his saddle, knocking the breath out of her, and urged his horse forward into the woods at a gallop. She was unable to scream as her sled collided with a tree and scattered her books everywhere.

The branches slapped her face and legs as they rode away from the road. She tried to hit one leg of her captor but could not muster much strength. The man stopped his horse and quickly tied her hands behind her back and again urged his horse forward. Martha thought she could see another rider following them. They were on an overgrown road that had been used before the new turnpike opened except the rider crossed some cutbacks and went straight up the mountain. They didn't stop except to tie a gag around her mouth and slow to a trot. The clack of their hooves could be heard if anyone was around on the turnpike boards as they trotted.

Wesley ran into the woods but soon realized that he couldn't catch up without a horse. Foard sent him back up the road toward the cluster of wagons. No horses were coming down with any wagons. Some of the people said they heard a noise in the woods going in the opposite direction.

Wesley ran up the hill and pointed into the woods. "They took Martha!" Patrick asked Curtis for his horse and a rifle. Curtis told him about the old road, and he headed into the woods in that direction. It took him awhile to find the old road and some fresh hoofprints. There were two horses and probably two men.

It took four hours to get down this part of the road, and Frederick was anxious to get back to the top and learn if anyone knew what had happened to Martha. A small number of horses had been led down ahead of the wagon and was waiting for all the men to go back up to help.

Foard said, "We will go off the trail when we meet a wagon coming down, and I will lead this packhorse with a pair of ropes. Someone will have to shuttle up and down to get ropes back to the top."

Lucy's cook wagon was coming next. Maybe someone would have news. Lucy told him what happened up top, and he just frowned. Frederick knew he could be more helpful at the bottom of the hill, gathering firewood to get coffee and some soup for the folks arriving with the goods they had been carrying. Frederick held Lucy tight, and they cried together.

Patrick stopped his horse when the trail disappeared. He dismounted and walked up and down both sides of the old road. Even with it becoming dark, he was relieved when he found some signs and followed them to the plank road. It wasn't possible to know which way they went on the turnpike, but he guessed it was east. They would have to stop at some point to rest the horses. Patrick headed for the stream where the wagons had previously stopped for a night, between two low hills. The moon shined against some smoke rising in the distance, and he dismounted. He tied his horse where it could feed and poured some water from his canteen into his hat for it to drink. Then he walked along the side of the road, making as little noise as possible with his rifle at the ready.

When they stopped, her feet had to be tied to stop her from kicking or running. They propped her against a tree and poured some water on her scratched face. Martha was scared and angry. *They gonna sell me back into slavery.*

"We should have some fun with this one after all our trouble," said Al as he unbuttoned her jacket and blouse, exposing her breasts. He cupped a hand around one breast and gave it a hard squeeze while starting to untie a rope holding her pants. Then he pushed her legs up so he could spread her legs with her feet still tied.

"Ah, man, we need to get movin'," said Bill shaking his head.

"I won't be long with this beauty."

"Damn it, we don't have time," Bill said, pulling Al away by his coat collar.

With her legs up, Martha managed to reach the knife with her hands still tied. She was holding the knife by the handle with the blade upright. She was thinking about how to cut herself free.

Al got to his feet and lunged at Bill, who knocked him aside with his rifle. Al tripped and fell backward on Martha. He landed with a groan.

At that moment, Patrick stepped out of the woods and said, "Drop your gun and cut her loose."

Bill turned toward Patrick with a cocked rifle. He said, "You can only shoot one of us. Put your gun down and we will let you go." Al groaned again, and Bill turned to see why. Patrick quickly fired. The unaimed shot hit Bill in the side and knocked him down. He tried to pick up his rifle when Patrick stepped on his hand.

The knife had struck Al's heart through his back. He didn't survive his fall. Bill's bleeding was stopped by stuffing strips of Al's shirt into the holes where the bullet went in and out.

They had no way to bury Al, so he was tied over Bill's horse. Bill rode with his hands tied to his saddle horn. Martha and Patrick rode while Patrick led Bill's horse.

It was early the next morning before they reached the small camp of four wagons still at the top of the mountain. Wesley had volunteered to stand guard and let out a yell when he saw them coming silhouetted by the rising sun.

Several men helped bury Al. Bill was tied and allowed to rest in a wagon.

Martha hugged Patrick. "How can I ever repay you for what you have done?"

"I suppose you should keep teaching us," Patrick said, turning and walking to his wagon.

Martha rode down the steep road with her arms around Wesley to a warm greeting by Frederick.

"Patrick and the knife Frederick gave me saved my life. I'm exhausted. I'll tell all after I get some sleep."

Blacks—free and enslaved—are denied the right to testify as witnesses in court cases.

Virginia Law (1705)

January 1949, Charleston, Virginia

Chapter 11
Blacks in Court

The last of the wagons got to the bottom of the steep mountain. The people just joining had little time to celebrate before they heard "Wagons, roll." Martha and Patrick were still sleeping, and others doubted they would be interested in a party. The rolling would be easier now that the snow days and the steep mountains with cutbacks were behind them. They were cautioned to be more careful than ever, but that advice was unnecessary. Their unhappy captive would be dropped in Charleston in a few days. They would be relieved not to have him around.

A mail rider slowed as he passed the wagons on a horse white with sweat. He chatted with Foard before galloping ahead. Mail riders passed their train in either direction about once a week and sometimes were a source of information and news. Horses were exchanged at toll booths and in stables at larger towns.

A day later, the rider arrived in Charleston. The news of the wagon train's closeness quickly spread through the town. As the wagons rolled into town late one afternoon, some locals were sitting on their porches, and others were standing on the wooden walkways in front of their homes. After a few wagons passed the sitting people, the people got up, shook their heads, and started inside. A woman picked up a broom and swept her porch with dirt flying in the direction of the wagons. One man had to drag a child who wanted to stay and watch. Their doors closed, and the freed people could see boarded-up windows. They felt rejected, and some feared that these hostile people would do something to hurt them. As they passed a shop, a sign appeared in a window that read, "*No Colored Served*," and next door was a shop with a sign saying, "*Everyone Welcome*." These signs perplexed the travelers. Meanwhile, a few people standing along the walks were waving and smiling.

At one point, the wagons passed a slave auction. The slaves were paraded naked under a porchlike roof that ran the length of the rundown grain storage building. Quakers and some other folks were protesting auctions by distributing pamphlets. The free people were upset by seeing the auction and feared that someone might try to put them up for sale.

Among locals who saw colored as human beings, there was even talk of becoming a new state if Virginia ever left the Union. These folks had put some firewood for campfires and hay for the animals in corrals at the far end of town.

The wagons were greeted by the sheriff and two deputies on horseback.

"We've been expectin' you," said the sheriff, dismounting, and his deputies did the same.

"I'm Dr. Patteson. This is Foard, my wagon master," he said as they walked to greet the sheriff.

The sheriff was a tall, slender man with a badge shining brightly on his vest. "I'm Sheriff Tuttle. You can park your wagons on the far end of town past the last building. You'll find a corral for the animals and firewood," said the sheriff.

"That's mighty friendly of y'all," said Dr. Patteson.

Tuttle said, "Not all agrees with me on lettin' you stop here. Half of the houses have no lamps showing, and the windows are shuttered. They don't even want to see your wagon train. Don't knock on their doors because they told me that would be considered trespassing."

Foard said, "We'll be careful and go as the sun rises. Any supplies we can get?"

"You're in luck. The supply store is open, and the owner is willing to sell you what he can," said the sheriff, pointing to a building sign halfway down the street on the left side.

"What about the bank?" asked Dr. Patteson.

"Nope, it's closed. They's afraid customers might leave if they dealt with you," Tuttle said.

Patrick was frustrated until Dr. Patteson said, "Very well. Patrick, get your guest for the sheriff." Head held high, Patrick marched to where Bill was leaning against a wagon and untied his harness and practically dragged him to the small group of men with whom they had been talking.

Dr. Patteson said, "This man was trying to steal one of our people until we caught up with him. His partner didn't survive the fight. He's buried along the pike. This one needs a doctor to check his wound. I cleaned and bandaged it, and the bleeding stopped long ago."

Tuttle said, "It's a crime to steal property. Since these are free colored, I don't know what the crime would be."

Bill said, "A bunch of them attacked us. She stabbed my partner."

Martha shouted, "He pushed his partner onto me. I was tied up and had gotten my knife out of my boot. He fell on me while I was still on the ground."

Bill said, "That's a far-fetched story and a damn lie. She ain't supposed to have a knife."

Tuttle asked, "Did any white man see what happened?"

Dr. Patteson said, "I'm afraid not."

Tuttle said, "I'm not a judge, but blacks can't be witnesses in court. Bill's word would carry more weight, depending on the judge. Seems that with what I heard, they saved your life. I'm going to call it a draw. Dr. Patteson, now, if you'll kindly be on your way in the morning . . ."

Foard said, "That's our plan."

Bill said angrily, "You ain't heard the last of this."

"Here are his horses and rifles," said Foard. "Don't want nobody accusin' me of bein' a horse thief."

"Take him to my office, boys, and get Doc Wilson to have a look at him," said Tuttle.

When the people in the train arrived at the other end of town, they were amazed at the welcoming they saw, including hay for the mules and goats and wood for fires. That evening during the campfire singing, some Quakers joined them. The locals were surprised when the singing included a well-known Quaker hymn.

Patteson announced, "We need extra guards tonight. Bill may be loose, and some of the locals are not too happy we're here."

The night passed quietly. The next morning, several local families came to the circle to watch the activities. Several ladies in long, plain brown dresses with matching bonnets showed up with hot buns and several buckets of scrambled eggs. Buns and eggs were the best breakfast the free people had enjoyed in a long time.

The freed people teams waved as they buried their latrines,

hitched mules, and loaded the wagons. The scouts, Foard, and Dr. Patteson returned to the train from the hotel, where they had comfortable beds and good food. When the train left the corral, the freed people were surprised at the cheers and applause. As the train started to roll away, a gathered small crowd of well-wishers sang another tune.

A child born to a Black mother in a state like Mississippi . . . has exactly the same rights as a white baby born to the wealthiest person in the United States. It's not true, but I challenge anyone to say it is not a goal worth working for.

Justice Thurgood Marshall

January 1848, Western Virginia

Chapter 12
Coming of Age

Several miles out of Charleston, the road had planks just past another toll booth, and the smooth ride continued. Today, Martha had planned to ask Annise some questions that might help her with Patrick. So, later in the day, Martha asked Annise to walk with her.

Martha knew Annise had a boyfriend named Thomas and had seen them kissing. Now, she wanted to know how it felt if a kiss was wanted. Her experience with Bil-Buck ducking away and Al forcing himself on her left her doubting it was ever good.

While they were walking together next to the cook wagon, Martha asked, "How old is Thomas?"

"He's fifteen," said Annise.

Only two years older, so I won't push the age difference, Martha thought, then she asked, "Do you ever like being kissed?"

Annise laughed and said, "That's a funny question."

Martha said, "Not in my experience."

Annise asked Martha what happened to her that she felt that way. After Martha explained the two experiences, Annise said, "Al jumping you was awful, but it sounds like Bil-Buck was afraid of being seen by someone."

Martha asked, "Who would he be afraid of?"

Annise said, "Another girl." Martha frowned.

Annise decided to try to give Martha the positive side of kissing. She explained that while holding hands sitting under a tree, the boy might tilt his head sideways and move toward your face. Martha was shocked . . . or thought she was until Annise explained that he might also put his hand on your breast.

"Oh!" Martha said, making a distasteful face. She didn't like it when Al had his hands on her.

Seeing Martha's look, Annise laughed and said, "Oh, you will like it very much when you get kissed and touched by someone you like."

"I hope someone treats me like that. You make it sound better," Martha said.

"I hope Patrick is not the 'somebody' you're thinking about," Annise told her.

"Why not?"

"He doesn't give you the time of day. You need to find someone who treats you like a queen."

"He saved me from Al and Bill."

"He just likes to fight."

Martha felt hurt by what Annise had said, but she knew there was some truth in it.

In the middle of the night, screams and sobs came from one of the wagons. Several flaps went up, and eyes peered into the darkness. Martha saw her daddy roll over, and he gave a small wave as the two women left the wagon. Martha knew that her momma helped other women have babies, but she had never been asked to help before. She was anxious about what she would have to do.

When the curious people saw Lucy and Martha near Juda's wagon, they closed the flaps and went back to sleep. Foard ran over with a pistol and talked with Lucy. Then he holstered his firearm and went back to his wagon.

Lucy climbed into Juda's wagon while Martha added some wood to coals still blinking from the cook's wagon fire. She knew to start with smaller pieces, and when they were burning, then add some bigger pieces that would be the core of the fire. She put a pot of water on to boil. Martha took Juda's two boys by their hands and started walking to her wagon.

Ben, one of Juda's boys, asked, "Why is Momma screamin'?"

"She's having a baby, but with my momma's help, she'll be fine," Martha said, hoping that was true.

The air was crisp and cold, and she could see her breath as they scurried to her wagon. The boys climbed into the wagon and found Martha's still-warm bedroll and crawled between the layers. When she got back, Nicey was making coffee over the fire.

Juda stopped screaming, and Martha climbed in the wagon to see if the baby had come. With the candlelight flickering in the wagon, she could see that her momma had given Juda a stick. As she watched, she could see Juda sitting up and heard her momma tell Juda to push, while helping Juda. After a minute or two, Juda leaned back against the side of the wagon.

"She doesn't have a man. How can she have a baby?"

"Ain't got to live with a man to make a baby. Just let a man sleep with you," said Lucy.

Martha, always curious, asked, "Who was the man?"

"Any of a dozen. She'll let any man sleep with her for a gift. Eat this bread, then start some coffee."

Later, Lucy handed Martha two towels and told her to dunk them in the boiling water, wring them out, and bring them back. When she returned with the hot towels, Martha watched as one foot appeared. Lucy said, "This is not good." The baby's bottom and other foot appeared. Pushing her hands inside Juda, Lucy tried to find the baby's head.

Seeing a blue leg, Martha felt queasy and worried that something was wrong.

Lucy looked defeated and wrapped the stillborn body in a towel. Martha and Lucy took the lifeless infant and the afterbirth in a bucket into the woods. They dug a three-foot-deep hole and were sweating profusely as they buried the baby and placed a large rock on the small mound. Then they buried the afterbirth about as deep, but somewhat away from the tiny body.

Walking back to their wagon, Martha said, "Momma, I'm never going to have a baby. It hurts too much, and the baby dies."

"When its head is first, it'll make it."

"I'm sorry the baby died," said Martha.

"I feel like I failed Juda," said Lucy. "I need to try to sleep."

There was a chill in the air, and large flakes were swirling around the wagons. Martha thought they looked like small angels.

Ohio enacted Black Laws aimed at discouraging settling in 1804 and 1807 that compelled blacks entering the state to post a bond of $500, guaranteeing good behavior and to produce a court paper as proof that they were free.

January 1849, Ohio River, Virginia Side

Chapter 13
Row, Row, Row Your Boat

The days of switchbacks, deep snow, and attacking pattyrollers allowed only traveling short distances and exhausted everyone, but the last couple of days of gently rolling hills on the new turnpike renewed their spirits.

The wagon train arrived at the Kenova Ferry. Everyone climbed down from their wagons to get a look at a free state. "Funny," said Patrick, "it looks like everywhere we've been."

They were stunned, looking at the river. The muddy brown Ohio had overflowed its banks and was full of rapidly moving sheets of ice on an otherwise smooth surface. A ferry was coming back from the Ohio shore with a colored man using a pole to push big pieces of ice away from the flatboat. Two men and a horse were on board, but otherwise, the ferry was empty and coming toward a dock at a steady pace.

Foard trotted up to Dr. Patteson's carriage and said, "I'm gonna send one cook wagon over first and you over second."

"How long is this going to take?" Dr. Patteson asked.

Foard guessed the rest of today and most of tomorrow. The ferry could only take one wagon at a time, and they could get four or five wagons across before dark. He had never seen this much ice flowing. Getting all the wagons across with that ice would complicate things.

They could see a horse walking on a treadmill and a paddle wheel turning. A rope helped keep the ferry on track. Under the ferry was a long, flat rudder that used the current to assist with forward motion.

After the ferry docked, the captain said, "You have brought a lot of colored to cross. I charge a dollar for each man, woman, and child. It costs two dollars for an animal and five for each wagon. The boat only holds one wagon at a time and no more than six people. If any whites want to cross, they will go first."

"What if our mules are on the treadmill?" asked Foard.

After spitting a wad of tobacco, the ferry captain said, "No charge for them, but I'll have to use my horse on the last wagon."

Dr. Patteson said, "I'll settle up when we are all across."

"I'll need cash up front," said the captain.

Dr. Patteson said, "I will pay you after every four wagons and the last set of three."

"Hows bout haf now and haf when dey is all over?" proposed the captain, pointing to the Ohio side.

"I'm afraid you won't do your job, and you are afraid I won't pay," smiled Dr. Patteson.

"Yep," said the captain.

"I'll pay for four now. Then, pay for groups of four, and after the final three," said Dr. Patteson.

"You gotta deal," said the captain, holding out his hand.

The shook hands, and Patteson headed for his cabinet. He

climbed into his buggy and opened the secret drawer in the side of the trunk. No one knew about the secret drawer. Dr. Patteson moved a couple of pieces of the side that unlocked a drawer. The chest was brand-new and had been protected during the trip. It had brass hinges and leather straps supporting the lid and drawers. The secret drawer opened with a strap across the top, hiding the crack in the cabinet.

Two mules were bridled in place on the treadmill, and two more for the cook wagon were practically dragged. The ferry was turned around by the captain and his colored helper using poles against the bottom of the river and ropes pulled by workers on a pair of docks.

Frederick and his two boys were put on three of the cook wagon's wheels. The ferry captain took the tongue. The colored ferry worker was already at one of the front wheels next to the brake lever. The cook wagon was rolled on the dock, then onto the ferry with the captain shouting, "Slow, slow. Now, pull the brake."

The colored man pulled the brake lever, grabbed blocks, and placed them in front and behind his wheel. The other three men looked around and grabbed blocks for their wheels. The mules were unhitched and required lashes to go onboard. They would be eager to get to the other side.

"What's your name?" Frederick asked the colored helper.

"Name is Irv," he said.

"Where you from, Irv?"

"I's from 'bama. Wher you'ens from?"

"Lynchburg, Virginni. We were freed three months ago and are on our way to Indiana," said Frederick.

"You'ens talk funny, but you'ens must be the luckiest darkies I eva met. Deys so many colored workin' on dis ole river dat nobody asks if we is free or runnin' and we makes good money. I has to keep my eye out for any pattyrollers, and when I sees one, I keep out of sight. I'm gonna buy my wife and chilen when I saves nough. You gonna see darkies on eva boat you see."

Each man took a pole and stood on the upriver side. Leslie had to be told which side was upriver. Irv was already in place with his pole and, with his hand, directed Frederick Jr. and Leslie to spread out. They were to put their pole on a piece of ice and walk it down past the paddle wheel. The bigger pieces took two men. It wasn't long before Dr. Patteson, now sitting on the driver's seat, saw a big chunk of ice coming toward the ferry, and he became alarmed. Before he could say anything, Irv had his pole on it and was maneuvering it along the side of the ferry. Irv signaled Frederick Jr. to help him. The two men walked along the boat. They were pushing hard and slipping a little on the wet ferry floor.

Leslie shouted, "I need help here," putting his pole on another big floating chunk.

Irv came to his rescue and said, "Don't push too hard on it. Dat only make it slip. Let ole man river hep. Let's take it for a walk."

The three men were busy most of the trip sliding pieces of ice to the back of the ferry.

Martha had jumped from her perch on the driver's board and climbed out the back of the wagon. She was holding onto the side of the wagon when a piece of ice the men missed bumped the side of the ferry and slid under the shallow craft, causing it to tip. Martha lost her grip, fell under the wagon, and began to slide toward the downriver side of the ferry.

Leslie, in the middle of the ferry, slid his pole toward her under the wagon. Martha reached for the pole and managed to hold it with one hand as her legs went over the side.

"Ahhhh," she screamed as her legs hit the frigid water. Her hand started to slide down the pole.

Irv jumped over the wagon tongue and, holding the rail, made his way toward Martha.

"Grab my arm," Irv said, wrapping one leg around a rail post.

When she had a good grip, he pushed off the post with one leg and slid both bodies to safety under the wagon.

Martha rolled to her side and put her arms around him. Shaking, she got to her knees and crawled from under the wagon. As she got to her feet, the ferry righted. The captain knew she was lucky. She would not have lasted long in freezing water. Dr. Patteson had never seen hypothermia, but he knew he would not have been able to help her.

"We's lucky it didn't break any paddles in the wheel. It takes a day to replace 'em," said the ferry captain.

Martha's mom threw a blanket around Martha and made her sit next to her in the back of the wagon.

As the ferry got close to the Ohio side, the mules were hitched. After what seemed like an eternity, the ferry dropped its front gate. The mules needed very little encouragement to head toward dry land.

The captain was pleased to get his money and hurried back to the ferry. When he reached the ferry, he said to Frederick Jr. and Leslie, "Do you want to work and help us get the other wagons across? I'll pay you each twenty-five cents a wagon."

The two young men looked at their father, who nodded his approval.

"Yes," they said in unison and climbed aboard.

Dr. Patteson shouted, "Bring my horse and carriage on the next trip."

They watched as the ferry was turned using the same setup as it had on the Virginia side. Frederick took the reins from Lucy, and Dr. Patteson sat on the board next to them. As they started up a road leading to the top of the riverbank, a man approached on horseback.

The man stopped next to Dr. Patteson. "I see you have three colored with you. They must be free, or you would be taking them the other way. That will cost you one thousand and five hundred dollars."

Dr. Patteson reached into his pocket and withdrew a copy of the will that he had retrieved from the secret drawer when he paid the ferry captain.

"I am the executor of this will, and according to the terms of the will, I will be taking them to Indiana," said Dr. Patteson in his calm, yet firm voice. "In fact, I'm escorting seventy-five colored to Indiana."

"Seventy-five colored?" asked the astonished tax agent.

Trying to assure him, Dr. Patteson said, "That is correct and all to Indiana."

The tax agent, removing his hat and scratching his head of thinning, greasy hair, said, "I ain't heard of sech a thin. I'll ask Colonel what he kens."

"We will be in camp until tomorrow night if your colonel wants to hear it from me," said Dr. Patteson.

The tax agent said, "Don't go no wheres 'til we git back." Then he yanked his horse around and galloped up the road.

"We've been dealing with all kinds of folks on this trip, and no one has said welcome yet," said Frederick, urging the mules up the gentle slope.

"Too bad Charleston is in Virginia," said Lucy.

A camp of a few wagons had been set up in an open field overlooking the river. Lucy fixed dinner last night and now breakfast. Some of the men walked to the edge of the steep slope and watched another wagon arrive. Then a group of four armed men rode into the partial circle of wagons.

Shouting, Dr. Patteson said, "What can I do for you?"

While dismounting near the buggy, a uniformed man said, "I'm the head of the tax office for this region. I was told that you have seventy-five colored coming to Ohio."

Dr. Patteson climbed down from his buggy. "We are on our way to Indiana, and I can show you the will that directs me to Indiana."

Not quite Dr. Patteson's height, the man said, "I'll have to see that will. Even then, I'm not sure you can go without the tax."

"Wait here. I'll get the will, and then we'll talk," said Dr. Patteson.

He climbed into the buggy, quietly opened the secret drawer, and removed one sheet of notes worth one hundred dollars.

"I'm Dr. Patteson, executor of the will, and I'm responsible for this wagon train," he said, holding out his hand.

"You can call me Reg," said the uniformed man, shaking Dr. Patteson's hand.

"Let's go for a walk, Reg, away from the wagons. Lucy, get some coffee and biscuits for our visitors," said Dr. Patteson.

Dr. Patteson led Reg toward a wooded area next to the wagons. A short distance into the woods, he stopped and opened the will inside his coat to protect it from the light rain that had started and said, "Here is what it says about our destination."

"I think I'll have to ask you to stay here until I contact the main office in Columbus and get their opinion. Your colored are gonna need last names now. I didn't see any in the will," said Reg.

Dr. Patteson put away the will and produced a folded sheet of banknotes worth one hundred dollars and asked, "Reg, maybe you don't need to check if this helps with your decision?"

Reg saw signed notes. He took the sheet, quickly refolded the notes, and slipped them under his coat.

"Well, that helps a lot. I think you are good to go when you are ready," he said.

Signaling with his hand toward the wagons, Dr. Patteson said, "After you, Reg."

Reg mounted his horse, and his men followed him, leaving

the wagons.

Foard accompanied the last wagon to their camp as it became dark. He rode over to Dr. Patteson and said, "That is the last of them. Is dinner ready? How did you do with the tax men?"

"Dinner is ready, and the tax man wasn't cheap, but we can roll in the morning," said Dr. Patteson.

Foard said, "I saw Bill and a sheriff on the road behind our wagons. The sheriff told me that he didn't have jurisdiction in Ohio, and they left. Maybe this rain will give up too."

After dinner, Dr. Patteson assembled the heads of the families and single men and women and told them they needed to decide on last names for their families and tell him in the morning.

Frederick talked only to Lucy about the family needing a last name. "Since I'm Master Warwick's son, we should take his name," Frederick said.

With a wry smile, Lucy said, "That would be most appropriate. I'm pleased to see you have accepted who your father was."

And be it further enacted, That any person who shall knowingly and willingly obstruct, hinder, or prevent such claimant . . . from arresting such a fugitive from service or labor, either with or without process as aforesaid, or shall rescue shall, for either of said offences, be subject to a fine not exceeding one thousand dollars, and imprisonment not exceeding six months . . .; and shall moreover forfeit and pay, by way of civil damages to the party injured by such illegal conduct, the sum of one thousand dollars for each fugitive so lost as aforesaid, to be recovered by action of debt.

Virginia Law

February 1849, Southwestern Ohio

Chapter 14
Where Are the Tracks for This Railroad?

It had been a sunny, warm, pleasant, late-winter thaw and uneventful day. The rolling hills made the travel easier, and they covered more miles than was possible in the mountains. A slender colored man in tattered clothes watched the train from a hiding place in the nearby woods. He squinted at the train and tipped his head, wondering what he was seeing. After watching most of the wagons pass, he approached the last wagon of the train.

"Where yu'all goin'?"

"To Indiana," Patrick said. "Where you headed?"

"Canada, but I lost the trail to safe stations. Do you know where it is?"

"Nope," said Patrick.

Martha and Frederick stopped walking and looked back at Patrick's wagon. As they did, a woman and young girl also stepped out of the woods and approached the people walking with the man. They were identified as the stranger's woman and daughter. They looked like they had been run over by a team of mules. Their clothing was torn and dirty. The little girl's arm was in a sling, apparently made from the man's shirt arm. Patrick told his sister to stop their wagon.

After a long silence, Martha said, "I'm Martha. Her arm looks funny."

"She fell and broke it. Almost got caught las' night cause of her moanin'. Can you hep?" the man asked.

Frederick said, "We'll be stopping soon, and there's a woman who is good with herbs who might be able to help her. Climb in this wagon until we stop for the night."

The three mysterious people were helped into Patrick's wagon and given some bread and water. They fell asleep soon after leaning back against the side of the wagon.

Lucy was known for treating all kinds of ailments with herbs that Dr. Patteson had shown her. She and Martha had gone with Dr. Patteson through fields, along streams, and into the woods in their searches for herbs. Dr. Patteson used them instead of bloodletting, and his patients were known to do better.

Lucy came around the wagon with a sack of dark green leaves, a piece of white cloth, and a jug of whiskey, and said, "Oh my, I bet that hurts."

With big eyes, the little girl nodded her head.

"Can you help?" asked her mother.

"I have some things that may help," said Lucy, climbing and turning to the injured girl. She asked, "What's your name? How old are you?"

"I'm Sadie, Rosie's mama. We wuz told not to use names. Are we safe with you?"

Lucy nodded.

"Her daddy's name is Jessie," said Sadie.

"I'm seven," Rosie said. "Will this hurt?"

Lucy ignored the question and began mixing some ground comfrey leaves in a tin cup with water and flour. The doughlike paste was spread on half of a cloth and enclosed by the other half.

"Get her to lean forward," ordered Lucy. Then, very softly, Lucy asked, "May I see your arm?"

When Rosie nodded, Lucy carefully took off the sling. Rosie started to cry.

"It's broken but did not break the skin. Dat is good," said Lucy. "Take a sip of this. It's strong. Don't spit it out. It's for pain."

Clearly taking charge, Lucy said, "Jesse, you hold Rosie by the shoulders, and Patrick, get a hold of her feet. More sips, girl."

Rosie did as told, and she relaxed a little. When Rosie had put the cup down, Lucy took her swollen red forearm and quickly snapped it in place. Rosie howled in pain but settled down when Martha gave her another gulp of whiskey.

Lucy wrapped Rosie's arm with the poultice and gently tied it to Rosie's arm. Two sticks were tied along the forearm, and her sleeve was pulled back down. By the time Lucy finished, Rosie had fallen asleep.

Lucy said, "I will change this poultice several times, but she should heal nicely. May I see your back, Jesse? I saw you wince when you moved."

"OK, but it isn't broken," he said, smiling while removing his shirt. His pants were tied on with a piece of rope.

"You must be hungry," said Lucy to Jesse. "Let me get you some bread and cheese."

Sadie said, "You are mighty kind, Lucy. Where are you from?"

They were pleased to tell these unfortunate strangers their story and their hopes for the future. The running people were amazed at all that would be done to get settled.

Foard rode to the wagon and asked, "I heard a scream. What happened?" Patrick explained what had happened and that everything was fine. Foard turned his horse and rode toward the buggy at the front of the line.

The exhausted couple leaned back against the side and fell sound asleep. Lucy, with Patience's help, changed the poultice several times. The poultices were hot when Martha removed them, but Sam's back was no longer red.

How could we stand against anti-black prejudice if we were willing to practice or condone a similar intolerance?

Jackie Robinson

February 1849, Southwestern, Ohio

Chapter 15
Closing the Gate

When they stopped rolling, Patrick jumped down from his wagon and walked briskly to Dr. Patteson's buggy. People were eating dinner and unhitching mules. The privy crews were digging shallow holes. Dr. Patteson signaled him to climb up.

"Foard tells me that three coloreds came out of the woods and got in the back of your wagon. Why did you let that happen?" asked Dr. Patteson.

"Their little girl had a broken arm, and I asked Lucy to help," said Patrick.

"Are they runaways?"

"Yes," said Patrick.

With a tight forehead, Dr. Patteson said, "By law, we are required to turn them in. There is a big penalty for aiding them to escape. They could put us all at risk."

Patrick, looking down, said, "We can hide them in our wagon. We will find a safe house."

Dr. Patteson wanted the whole community to know about this and make their opinions known. He called a meeting of all the men over sixteen and asked what they thought we should do.

Patrick was surprised at Dr. Patteson's wanting input from anyone besides Foard, and he worried how that would turn out. It seemed to Patrick that Dr. Patteson would have sent them away, if not turn them in.

With a cocked head, Patrick asked, "Why you asking us what we think?"

Dr. Patteson replied, "You will soon be making decisions for yourselves. Hopefully, they won't all be this dangerous."

The family of runaways slept until the wagons formed a circle and stopped. The lack of noise startled them awake. Lucy pulled Rosie close to her. Martha was watching from the inside of the circle.

Jesse said, "Are we stopped for the night?"

"Yes, we are. This was a good day for rolling," said Patrick.

"What can I do to help?" asked Jesse.

"Finding and chopping firewood is always needed, if you are up to it," said Patrick. "Why don't you tag along with Frederick Jr. and give him a hand and take this ax."

Frederick walked along to watch the team of men who were now forming to find firewood in a nearby grove of leafless trees. Frederick Jr. found a dead tree that was still standing, and Jesse and Patrick started to cut it down by taking turns on one side of the tree.

"Some folks are concerned that your family is on the trail with us," said Patrick.

"We don't want to cause any trouble. Soon as we find a safe house, we'll be gone," said Jesse. "Let me cut on the other side a bit, and we can drop this dead log right between those trees."

Jesse moved around the tree and watched as big chips began to fly.

"Timber," shouted Patrick as the tree creaked loudly and fell where Jesse had said it would. Two men who had been working on another tree joined Patrick and Jesse, and each man took a different large branch and began cutting pieces short enough for the cooking fires. Martha was cutting the smaller branches into a pile she had started. She tied the pile with a rope and started back to the wagons. Frederick loaded Jesse with six pieces of freshly cut wood, and he gave Patrick a similar load. Then Frederick picked up several branches, and the three men headed back.

Jesse said, "Maybe we should be on our way."

Frederick said, "You need a hot meal and to wait until you hear opinions in the meeting tonight. There is no one around here. We haven't found a safe house."

As they entered a loose circle, Patrick said, "Jesse, take your load to Lucy. Mine to the other fire. Martha, bring us some of that kindling."

After Jesse had dropped his load of firewood where Lucy pointed, he said, "I'm going for another load."

Patrick said, "Not tonight. You are pretty good with an ax, and you have obviously cut down trees before. Gathering firewood is a daily task for us, and I'm grateful for your help."

"I feel I'm not doing much to repay all you are doing for my family," said Jesse.

When the cooking fires were reduced to glowing embers and a few burning logs, a group of men was waiting for Dr. Patteson. Fog was beginning to form, and it mingled with the smoke from the fires. The chill of the evening was coming quickly.

Jesse and his family were in Patrick's family wagon that was far from the meeting. Patrick had advised Jesse to stay back. He thought it would be better for the others to see this forlorn family but feared that such a move might backfire. Dr. Patteson walked up to the group with his back to one of the dying fires. He looked like a giant with the fire creating a light that outlined his form but darkened his features.

"We may have a problem," he began. "A runaway family has joined our wagons, and if anyone finds them, we'd be punished."

The men became restless, and some were whispering.

Speaking loudly, Dr. Patteson said, "A federal law was passed in 1783 to punish anyone helping a runaway slave. The fine for helping is one thousand dollars."

The men looked at each other, and some of them exhaled purposely, giving voice to their concern.

"Would everyone be punished or just me?" asked Patrick.

"I don't know," answered Dr. Patteson.

This response did little to reassure the few who were clearly agitated.

Charles, one of the single men who had been hired out most of the time, said, "We are free. Ain't no sense in risking our freedom."

Harry asked rhetorically, "We don't know these people. Why should we help 'em?"

Leah said, "I have a large family with three young children. I'm hesitant to take risks that might harm them."

John said, "I don't agree. We can easily cover for these people. Ain't no one gonna count in Ohio."

Ben said, "Yea. John is right."

Lindsey, representing Nicey's family, said, "I'm sure Mom would think we should take care of these people. 'Sides, Jessie is good with an ax. He ain't gonna be no burden."

Patrick said, "So some of us think that since we have our freedom, we should close the gate. I think we should help others like us. They are as desperate for their freedom as we used to be. I'll take them in my wagon and hide them in the storage space under the floorboards. If, God forbid, someone discovers them, I will claim sole responsibility and say that none of you knew anything."

The crowd went silent. Charles said, "Dr. Patteson, would we be safe?"

Tilting his head to one side and frowning, he said, "It might work."

Patrick said, "Thank you, Dr. Patteson, for listening. It'll be only a day or two."

The men respected Patrick and knew his word was good. The final vote only had two nays.

I was the conductor of the Underground Railroad for eight years, and I can say what most conductors can't say; I never ran my train off the track, and I never lost a passenger.

Harriet Tubman

February 1848, Southern Ohio

Chapter 16 They Found a Train Station

It was almost sunset, two days after the runaway family climbed into Patrick's wagon. Foard shouted, "Wagons, whoa." Foard had seen an unlit lantern on the back of the house and hoped that was the sign they were looking for.

Foard stayed out of sight and was ready, if needed. Patrick walked quickly across the road and followed a path to the house. He knocked firmly, so he was sure he could be heard. The door opened, and a woman, surprised by a black man at her front door, grabbed Patrick firmly by his coat, pulled him into the house, then slammed the door. Patrick stumbled and fell to the floor.

Without getting up, he said, "I thought this was a safe house."

"It is. The lantern ain't lit 'cause I'm being watched. I left some food out there. After dark, sneak out there and hide under the board in the privy," said the grey-haired, stocky woman in a plain dress.

"It's not for me. I'm Patrick Weaver, a free man. I'm with that wagon train across the way."

"I hope you're not going to report me," said the woman, crossing her arms and stepping back, spreading her feet.

Patrick thought the woman looked like she might be ready to fight. Getting to his feet slowly, he spun when he heard the door creak behind him. Foard came in with a whip in his hand.

Patrick shouted, "No need for that, Foard."

The woman had that surprised look on her face again and said, "Who do you think you are barging in?"

Patrick said, "He's the wagon master for our group. We're on our way to Indiana."

"I thought you were capturing Patrick," said Foard, rolling his eyes and laughing while tying his whip to his belt.

Patrick saw the woman relax, and he said, "We got some runaways. Can you help them on their way to Canada?"

The woman thought for what seemed like an eternity. Then she said, "Tell me who you are."

Foard said, "I am taking seventy-five free people to Indiana. We will only camp here one night and can pay for the use of your field. By sunrise tomorrow, you won't know we were here."

The stout woman explained that she was being watched, and she had two hidden already. More would be even more dangerous. It was a little past noon, two days after the runaway family had disappeared into Patrick's wagon.

Fearing a body count, Foard said, "Are there any towns between here and the next station?"

"No, but there is one a few miles past," said the woman.

Foard said, "I guess we can make this work."

The woman said, "That many men using my privy will help it look legitimate."

"I'm glad you didn't throw me in the privy," said Patrick.

"I was about to do just that when you showed up at my door," the woman said, smiling.

Patrick knew who he could ask that would not tell anyone else in the wagon train. He was thinking about Frederick, Wesley, Jesse, and two single men.

They walked casually back to the circle, then Foard mounted his horse and rode over to where the scouts had dismounted. Patrick rounded several men to help with this chore.

The pattyrollers were distracted by one of the scouts who were told an extra privy was needed. They walked with torches and appeared to enjoy having the nice extra privy and laughed a little while walking back and forth. They were told not to look around and not to hurry.

Patrick waited for a short time, then said, "Any questions?"

"Won't the pattyrollers see different men coming and going?" asked Jesse.

"They think we all look alike," said Patrick.

Patrick went first with Jesse and Wesley. They took the lantern in the back and lifted the lid of the two-hole privy. The two men in hiding appeared frightened but relaxed a little when they saw two colored arms extend to help one up. After both men were up, they were told where they would be hiding.

"Did I die and go to slave heaven?" one man asked.

"No. Every day, we thank our master who freed us."

They left the temporary space across from the watched station and traveled until the sun was on the horizon. The following day, the wagon train left early. Near sundown, they found the next station and made camp at sunset in a nearby field. After negotiations, they learned that the two men from the privy and Rosie's parents could hide, but the child had to stay with the wagon train. It would be necessary to crawl about twenty feet. There was no way to get a child with a broken arm into the hiding space.

This was devastating news. Their options were not good. Stay together, become a family on the run, or leave Rosie with the wagons. They asked if Rosie could stay and were told absolutely. The parents kissed the sleeping child goodbye and asked that she be told they loved her, and they would someday come back for her. Jesse and Sadie knew Rosie would be better off with the wagon train families. Jessie had to put an arm around Sadie and forced the sobbing mother to leave.

Dr. Patteson hurriedly said, "Go to the back door and someone will let you in. They have a hidden space on the third floor, and you will be indoors until you are ready to travel further. They asked me if I could see where the door was to the crawl space, and I could not. You will be safe."

One of the men said, "Thank you all, and God bless."

The four runners crouched low and all but disappeared in the darkness. They followed the Quaker woman up three flights of stairs and watched as she moved a cupboard away from the wall. A low door opened into a narrow crawl space that ended in a large attic room with a small window at one end. They understood that a knock on the wall would be a signal for one of them to retrieve some food by the door. There were blankets and some warm clothes for them to use. The only heat was from the chimney. A signal would be given when it was safe to leave for the next station. They would be transported to the next station in a wagon with a false floor covered with hay. Even if a pattyroller stabbed the hay with a pitchfork, it would only hit wood protecting the people.

Part III

A new community on Indian Lake Ohio How much damage can a damn do?

Hoosier state voters in 1850 adopted Article 13, which decreed in part that "No negro or mulatto shall come into or settle in the State, after the adoption of this Constitution."

https://www.in.gov/history/3117.htm

March 1849, Bellefontaine, Ohio

Chapter 17
Home Sweet Home?

The wagon train made camp just outside Bellefontaine near Indian Lake. Another week of travel lay ahead to get to Indiana. Then, no one knew how long it would take to buy land and get settled. Colored families heading east out of Indiana told them that they would not be welcome because Indiana was going to pass legislation so that no more colored could cross its borders.

Dr. Patteson, Foard, and the two scouts left the camp that night for Scott's Tavern in town. Frederick had asked to go along and was told the tavern was for whites only. So much for a free state mused Frederick. The tavern had acquired the smells of sausage frying and a piano being played as a busy place of hospitality and trade.

The four strangers sat at a table by themselves. One of the scouts moved toward a table where a woman in a long, red dress with a low-cut top with exposed shoulders was seated by herself. She crossed her legs as he approached, exposing her stockings that partially covered her thighs. She pulled out a chair for him, and they immediately began talking and laughing. After a signal from the woman, two drinks were poured at the table by the bartender, and the bottle was left.

Foard joked, "I hope he can find his way back to the wagons." The men laughed among themselves but looked away from the developing scene.

Foard said, "The folks are tired of travelin' and afraid of not being wanted. Maybe we could find farmland near here."

A paunchy, balding man in a suit and tie approached their table.

"I'm Lionel Bateson. If you are headed to Indiana, you might not be let in. Would you consider land here? You don't need to go any farther than Indian Lake. There's good bottomland with black soil. Darker than the darkest darkie you have in your wagon train," he said, chuckling at his play on words.

"How do you know I have a wagon train?" asked Dr. Patteson, a little surprised by the man's observations.

"The whole town is talking about the colored wagon train that came through today, and I saw you from my office," Lionel said.

"Sit down and tell me about your property," said Dr. Patteson, while waving the back of his hand toward his men.

"What are you drinking?" asked Lionel as he took the seat next to Dr. Patteson.

"Whiskey," Patteson said, picking up his almost empty glass.

"Let me buy you another drink," said Lionel, signaling the bartender to bring a bottle.

"Why not," said Dr. Patteson.

Lionel poured two generous drinks for Dr. Patteson and himself and asked, "Tell me what you might need in the way of land."

"I'm responsible for a dozen families and seven more single folks.

I need to buy enough land for them to support themselves. One hundred acres would be about right," Dr. Patteson explained.

"If you might consider the farming community of Goodland on the far side of Indian Lake rather than Indiana, your trek is over," Lionel said. "I too represent an estate whose family would like to sell one hundred acres of land they inherited. There isn't a farmer in the bunch, and they just want to get rid of it soon. So, I think they would sell for less than the current average of fifty dollars an acre if you were to make a good offer," explained Lionel, pouring Dr. Patteson another drink while just sipping from his own glass.

Dr. Patteson said, "I'll have to take your word on price per acre. How does forty dollars per acre sound? And what about the per-head tax?"

Dr. Patteson was not aware that the Ohio government was considering repealing the tax, but Lionel was.

"I think the land and store accounts would cover the tax liability, and I'll arrange that with the courthouse," Lionel said.

Foard was sent to the camp that evening to meet with the men. He explained what was possible and found they were supportive of not having to travel further and settling nearby.

The next morning, Dr. Patteson and Foard were in the office of Attorney Bateson, who had agreed to help with the purchase of land for the freed people with two conditions. First, it could never be known that he was involved. Second, his fee would be double. Dr. Patteson had become accustomed to extra costs every time he turned around.

Foard said, "Folks sure do make extra money off your colored."

Dr. Patteson, with one eyebrow raised, said, "They are not mine.

I will have no responsibility for them after we get them settled."

Foard said, "You have done your best to help them. They made it clear that they didn't want to go where they weren't wanted. Indian Lake sounded like Indiana to some of them anyhow."

"Good morning, gentlemen. Sorry to keep you waiting," said Lionel, entering the office. "No one knows you're here?"

"The free colored knows. They don't have any particulars and certainly no names," said Dr. Patteson.

"Fine, fine, fine, as agreed. There is a large parcel of land, about 100 acres, that should be big enough to start your people in farming, and there are enough trees for building cabins. The owners are willing to sell at your offer of forty an acre."

As Dr. Patteson handed Lionel banknotes totaling four thousand dollars, he wondered, *Am I being swindled? But the land and tax settlement solves the last of my big problems. I will be free of this commitment and maybe richer.*

Lionel asked for one thousand more in case the bank wouldn't honor the face value of the notes. Dr. Patteson understood the issue. He also planned to put enough money in the General Store accounts to support each family or person for a year. The accounts would vary by family size or household size. The rest of the money he would keep for his administrative expenses he might encounter on the way home or closing the estate.

"The owner wants to be anonymous also," said Lionel.

"I'd be celebrating after a good sale," said Dr. Patteson.

"It will all be kept quiet, and the papers will only say the land has been sold to John Warwick," replied Lionel.

"Will the colored be bothered by folks around here?" asked Dr. Patteson.

"If they stay to themselves and don't cause no trouble, they won't," advised Lionel. "I have prepared some papers for you to sign," he continued, rummaging in his briefcase.

"What happens next?" said Dr. Patteson.

"I will file these papers in the courthouse today, and the land is yours," said Lionel.

"Actually, the land will be theirs, and I will help them divide it into parcels," said Dr. Patteson.

"It is all yours, er . . . theirs, now," said Lionel.

Foard and Dr. Patteson rode back to where the wagons had set up camp, where Dr. Patteson called for a meeting as they stopped at Frederick's wagon.

"I want to tell everybody some very good news," said Dr. Patteson, hoping they would be satisfied with the purchase. Frederick and Frederick Jr. set out to assemble the people around a campfire. Word spread quickly through the camp, and in only a few minutes, the freed people gathered to hear from Dr. Patteson. He climbed into the back of one of the open wagons, and as soon as he faced the assembled throng, they became very still.

"You are home," he began. He observed many puzzled looks and decided he should elaborate on his statement. "Today, I bought one hundred acres of land near here for you to build cabins and begin farming."

The next morning, as the wagons started rolling toward their new land, the celebration among the people began again like it did on the first morning of the trek. The people singing, banging on pots with spoons, and even Banjo Boy's repaired instrument were now part of the celebration. The dogs at farmhouses they passed contributed to the din with howling. While the houses were far apart on this back road, people came out and sat on their porches. A few walked along Dr. Patteson's carriage and asked what was happening, and he supplied the standard explanation he had used so many times on the trail.

As the wagons formed a circle for the night, three men rode out to find the stakes marking the boundary of their land. One stake was near the circle. Much of the land had been cleared for farming but had been idle for a year. The land was flat, and they could see the three riders. One rider less than a quarter-mile away to the west waved a scarf. Another disappeared in a wooded area to the north while the third waved his scarf southwest. Their cabins would be built from that wood. Small lakes south of their land were sparkling in the sunset. One was close to their property.

Wesley took a shovel and dug into the dirt. Much to everyone's surprise, the earth was dark brown. They knew their vegetables would grow well in soil like this, unlike the orange clay where they came from that limited what would grow. This land and the nearby lake would serve them well.

That night, they celebrated with singing and dancing. Patteson and his men went back to Bellefontaine to a hotel. The freed people didn't know what could happen.

We allow our ignorance to prevail upon us and make us think we can survive alone, alone in patches, alone in groups, alone in races, even alone in genders."

- Maya Angelou

March 1849, Goodland, Ohio

Chapter 18
Home, Sweet Home

The first morning on their new land, the people were in awe and overwhelmed with what had to be done. From their land, they could see several small lakes. Dr. Patteson arrived around noon and met with the men and helped them elect a mayor and sheriff. Frederick was their unanimous choice for mayor, and Patrick won, hands down, to be the sheriff. They were given a list of groups to form to build the cabins, including men and women, to cut trees, prepare logs, and drag logs for different cabin sites.

One group was assigned a wagon to quarry flat rocks from the north fork of the Great Miami River. It was the closest possible place to find the stones. A group was assigned to find exposed rocks on a hillside that were more likely to be dry for the fireplaces. The last group of men was assigned to find cedar trees near the river.

These would be used to make shingles for the roof.

The women frowned when they were assigned to groups to make clay mud. When they understood that their product was critical for sealing the logs after they were in place, they smiled. Frederick assigned Juda to be in charge of the mud groups. The women had to dig holes away from the lake and river until they hit the clay they wanted. Several barrels and buckets of water were used to mix the clay into a muddy consistency. The gooey mix was delivered to a new cabin site.

Twenty-four sets of hinges for two doors per cabin and twelve windows, one for each cabin, were on order by Dr. Patteson. Boards had also been ordered to make the cabin floors. Sam and a couple of men would take three wagons and get these materials from a lumber mill near Bellefontaine. Sam would be needed to appease the mill owner who wouldn't sell to colored. Frederick, the men, and Dr. Patteson walked around and made stakes for where the new log cabins would be placed. The cabins would be a safer distance apart than where they had been living.

Frederick said, "You have given this a lot of thought, Dr. Patteson. I'm willing to take it from here."

Frederick told Martha and Annise to look after the youngest children. Lucy and Nicey were to keep their cook wagons going for meals every day.

The families and singles were shown their parcel of land, and the head of the family staked out the house. They finished at the site and returned to work in their groups. A load of rocks was delivered to the first cabin site, along with several trimmed logs that had been sawed to various lengths according to the plan Patteson provided. The large stones formed an outline of the cabin. Notches were chopped into each log. The number of people working on various tasks made the work go fast. As the day progressed, several cabins began to take shape.

During a break, Martha said quietly to Frederick, "He didn't spend all the money on us."

Frederick responded, "He did what Master Warwick's will directed him to do—moving us here, buying land for us, and giving us supplies for a year. I am feeling healthy and glad to be free. Dr. Patteson has done for us what few, if any, other whites would have done. Forget the numbers on this and get back to work."

A game was organized for the kids to find something from the woods near their new cabin and share it with others in the group. The older children were paired with younger children to help them play the game. They found beautiful stones, ferns that didn't grow on the plantation, and some bird feathers. Marigolds, mayapples, and purple cress spring flowers were popular finds.

The mothers with babies had gathered in one wagon and were worried about the work involved in setting up their new homes.

Nicey and Lucy fixed a stew for the noon meal for the workers, including the mud women. Everyone laughed at the mud women, who, by now, looked like mud statues. They sat on logs inside the circle of wagons. Annise and Martha did the best they could with getting the toddlers in their charge to eat. Some of them would only eat potatoes or meat and not the vegetables.

"I guess they are exercising their freedom," said Martha.

"Let's not waste what they don't want," said Annise.

Martha and Annise decided to walk the children around the newly started cabins. The children were told to hang onto a rope, with Martha leading and Annise following. At one foundation, the men were taking a break as the kids lined up along the first layer of stones that would form the foundation.

Bil-Buck said to his little brother, "Hello, Randal. This will be your new home in a few days." He picked up his young brother, and while walking around the stones, he started laughing. "Randal, you won't move here until we have a roof over your head. You will have a new mother too."

Martha was stunned. "Bu-bu-bu, who's that?"

Before Bil-Buck could answer, George said, "You are standing near the front door, and those extra stones are the foundation for the fireplace," pointing to an open space.

Anthony added, "You might like to know that the door and window will face south to let in the sunshine. The fireplaces will be built on the east end so that the smoke and sparks blow away from the roof. The wind is usually from the west. As you may recall, it was in our faces while on the trail."

"Will the cabins have dirt floors?" asked Annise.

"No, we will build a wooden floor using these stones and some logs we are sitting on as support for the floor," said Bil-Buck.

Randal asked, "Where will I sleep?"

Bil-Buck answered, "That is a good question that each family will have to answer. That second rectangle on this end of the big room will be a separate bedroom for the parents and maybe a baby. Some folks will sleep in an attic loft and have to watch their heads coming and going, and others will sleep in a corner of the big room. This cabin will be typical of all our cabins because Dr. Patteson only gave us one plan to follow," explained Bil-Buck.

Martha's eyes had watered up, and she couldn't talk, so Annise took charge. "Thank you for the tour. We need to get our bosses back to the wagon for a nap. I may take one myself." Martha knew she wouldn't sleep.

As the week progressed, the cabins seemed to appear from nowhere. The twenty-six men and nine women in different groups were able to build a cabin a day. The shingle roofs would be the last to finish, and the stone and log crew joined the shingle crew. The new village of fourteen cabins and one larger one-room cabin was finished in a week.

Dr. Patteson and the three men arrived early one day. Nicey and

Lucy had made pancakes for breakfast, and a table had been set for the four white men. When everyone finished eating, they lined up at the special table to thank the men for their care of them on the journey.

One toddler at the end of the line said, "Tank you, Woctor Great Man."

Frederick folded a sheet of paper and stuffed it in his pocket. He announced, "My thanks couldn't have been said better. Randal has stolen my speech."

Amid laughter and applause, he added, "You are Great Men, Dr. Patteson, Foard, Ben, and Curtis. You have delivered us to freedom."

Curtis took the driver's seat of the buggy, and Dr. Patteson climbed aboard. Lucy and Nicey placed a basket of freshly baked breads on the floor of the buggy. "God bless you all, and good luck," shouted Dr. Patteson as his buggy started down the road home.

Frederick led them in singing:

"A charge to keep I have,
a God to glorify,
a never-dying soul to save,
and fit it for the sky.
To serve the present age,
my calling to fulfill,
O may it all my pow'rs engage
to do my Master's will!"

The four white men waved their hats in acknowledgment.

Slaves who converted to Christianity and were baptized were not freed from slavery.

Virginia Law (1667)

Spring, 1850, Goodland, Ohio

Chapter 19
Rock and Roll on Sunday

Their dog's barking alerted the Warwick family that a wagon was approaching. It stopped near their cabin, and someone knocked at the door. When Frederick opened the door, a tall, thin colored man in a fine black suit with a white shirt and black bow tie greeted him. Behind him was a wagon full of people humming.

The man dusted off his shoulders and said, "I'm Reverend James King from the African Methodist Episcopal Brook Church in Cincinnati. We, that is, my family and some friends, want you to consider forming your own AME church," Reverend King said, holding out his hand to Frederick.

As they shook hands, Martha slipped out the door and smiled as a group of people standing in the wagon greeted her.

"AME?" Frederick said, still puzzled but relieved to meet another minister.

"African Methodist Episcopal. There are numerous AME churches in colored communities. We are popular in cities like Cincinnati, Philadelphia, and Boston. It's our own church. I'm sure you know the churches white folk attend don't want our kind around. Even when we worship the same Jesus," explained Reverend King.

Frederick asked, "Why did you come to my cabin?"

Reverend King said, "Some folks in town said that you were the mayor and, more importantly, the pastor for this community. You are the person who can make things happen."

The people in the wagon were humming a peppy tune. A young girl who had waved to Martha was signaling her to come over to the wagon. *Why not? The humming is beautiful.* The girl put down a hand, and Martha climbed into the open wagon by stepping on a spoke of the wheel near the hub and next to the edge of the wagon as she had done many times on their journey.

"My name is Ashley. My dad is talking to that man. Do you like to sing?"

Proudly, Martha said, "That's my dad. Yea, I love to sing. I can read too."

The wagon had benches with pillows for the group while they were rolling. One of the older women in the wagon moved to one side in the middle of the wagon. Martha wondered what would happen next. She found out quickly as Ashley picked up the hymnal and held it so Martha could see.

Ashley whispered, "When the flags go up, the notes go higher, and when the flags go down, the notes go lower."

They were standing at one end of the first row. Next to Ashely was a young boy. He elbowed Ashley in the ribs, and she pinched his arm. *Just like my brothers*, though Martha. Their mother's raised eyebrow restored order. Nine people formed two rows.

Ashley took Martha's arm and began swaying from side to side. Just a little at first and then more. The woman facing the nine people in the wagon lifted her arms and began making flowing gestures. Martha saw Ashley point to words on the page, and Martha heard the most beautiful voices burst into song.

"Our bondage it shall end, by and by, by and by.
Our bondage it shall end, by and by
From Egypt's yoke set free.
Hail glorious jubilee.
And to Canaan we'll return, by and by, by and by.
And to Canaan we'll return, by and by.
And when to Jordan's floods we are come, we are come,
And when to Jordan's floods, we are come,
Jehovah rules the tide, and the waters he'll divide,
And the ransom'd host shall shout, We are come."

Martha did her best to sing along and watch the flags over the words go up and down. Mostly, she listened to Ashley's voice and imitated the tone she heard. Ashley smiled nicely to Martha, and Martha had an incredible feeling of joy and comfort as she swayed with the wagon full of people.

Lucy, Frederick Jr., and Wesley came outside to the front of the cabin. Lucy had the most beautiful smile on her face. She didn't smile very often.

Frederick and Reverend King had stopped their discussion and were listening to the music.

Several families had heard the singing and were coming to see what was happening. Bil-Buck came holding a baby with Jane on his arm. Martha knew Bil-Buck had a partner but had not seen them before as a family. She focused on the music in front of her.

Pleasant, with Patrick trailing behind, also came to see what was happening.

Reverend King announced, "It looks like our choir has a new

member. What we would like most is to have everyone sing with us tomorrow. I will give a short sermon explaining the AME church. Of course, everyone is invited to visit us in Cincinnati."

Lucy disappeared and reappeared with a jug and glasses. She announced, "Lemonade for everyone. Please come into the shade." Wesley was afraid at first that she had brought out the jug of rum that her dad tried to keep hidden.

Ashley and Martha jumped down from the wagon, and Ashley led her over by her father, and they both stood so they could hear.

Reverend King asked, "Do you have a barn?"

Frederick bagged, "We have a cabin we use as a school."

Reverend King asked, "How many people are here in this community?"

Patrick said, "We have seventy-five who were on the plantation, and we lost one and gained one. We hide the runners, feed them, and point them to the next station."

How different things were since Patrick's family hid a running family while on the trail. When they built their cabins, several families added rooms that looked like firewood shelters with low roofs, and outdoor barns with hidden spaces behind pens and under staircases inside the cabins. Now, hiding folks on the run was almost routine. If a runner were seen along the road, he would be picked up and dropped at an empty shed. It was easier to hide without dogs this far from plantations.

The community celebrated for a week when they learned that the five-hundred-dollar tax on free colored coming to Ohio was repealed, and colored were allowed to have guns. That made it easier for the community to take in new people. They were helped to buy land, build cabins, and find jobs. Everyone knew that Indiana would not allow free colored to move there, so more were staying in Ohio.

Only a few of the people in the community were unhappy that the others were risking so much to help escaped slaves. At first, angry-looking pattyrollers came around. When shown manumission papers and saw colored men with guns, they galloped away. Now, such unwanted visitors were a rare occurrence, but everyone was still careful.

Reverend King announced, "If the weather holds, I would like to have an outdoor service typical of AME worship tomorrow. Then we'll see what you think about a church of your own."

Martha blurted out, "Will we get to sing that song again?"

Reverend King said, "My, yes. That is everyone's favorite. We brought some extra songbooks to leave."

By now, many people had gathered to see what was happening.

Ashley's mother stood and signaled her small choir to rise again. Ashley took Martha's arm and pulled her in with the others. With a wave of her arms, the choir started on another song.

"We are very grateful for your acceptance of our intrusion," said Reverend King.

Reverend King's wife said, "We brought some hams and biscuits and will share them after the service tomorrow."

"Tell me about your school," said Reverend King, between bites of chicken pot pie that evening at the dinner table.

Frederick said, "Well, let me introduce our teacher to you," pointing to Martha.

Martha's eyelashes went down as she tried to suppress a grin.

"You are young to be a teacher," said Elizabeth, Reverend King's wife.

Lucy said, "She started teaching at night around the campfires during our wagon train trip here."

"I enjoy teaching," said Martha.

Frederick added, "Our master, John Warwick, rest his soul, encouraged everyone to learn from each other."

He elaborated, "On the trail, she started with some of the children. Many adults listened to her teaching and asked if they could join. It wasn't long before Martha had several small groups every night. The older men and women were ashamed at first, but Martha's use of praise for every effort encouraged them. That smile of hers won the hearts of many of the older people."

"Dad helped me a lot with ideas for teaching, and he encouraged some of the older men and women to give it a try. Now, we have a school, and I teach the children in the morning and the older folks in the afternoon," said Martha.

"Do you get paid?" asked Ashley.

"Our family eats well because many of the families in Martha's school pay her with eggs, vegetables, and even fish from the lake," said Wesley.

Lucy smiled and nodded at Frederick.

Martha confessed, "Sometimes, I can't believe that people want to pay me to share what I know. I like to teach because I love to learn new things to share."

The next morning, they started with a gathering period, then encouraged people to greet each other. After that, they were directed to turn inward for some spiritual meditation. Without an organ or piano, the choir would hum a hymn. After they gathered, Reverend King said, "This is the day the Lord hath made; let us rejoice and be glad in it."

Frederick delivered the opening prayer. Next, they sang a hymn of praise to God. Reverend King announced that they would not take up a collection this morning, but he considered the people there a gift to God.

Ashley said, "This is from the Old Testament and Acts 37:7." Then she read:

"This is that Moses, which said unto the children of Israel, A prophet shall the Lord your God raise up unto you of your brethren, like unto me; him shall ye hear. This is he, that was in the church in the wilderness with the angel which spake to him in the mount Sina, and with our fathers: who received the lively oracles to give unto us."

Reverend King read from Matthew 16:18:

"I say also unto thee, that thou art Peter, and upon this rock I will build my church; and the gates of hell shall not prevail against it."

"That is from Matthew and perfect for wanting to start a church," said Frederick.

Smiling, Reverend King said, "Exactly. It is AME's motto. I will say 'God our Father, Christ our Redeemer, Man our Brother' and give a brief sermon about the church and the importance of God and Christ in our lives. I'm going to say a few words, and if something touches you, say 'Amen.'"

Ashley whispered to Martha, "Let's find a place to sit. His idea of a few words may be a lot of words."

In California, there are huge problems because of dams. I'm against big dams, per se, because I think that they are economically unfeasible. They're ecologically unsustainable. And they're hugely undemocratic.

Arundhati Roy

Spring, 1850, Goodland, Ohio

Chapter 20
Goodland or Badland?

The Ohio Canal Board was taking a suggestion from a representative of the Bellefontaine community. "We want to provide the Miami-Erie Canal with more water. It can easily be done by raising the height of the existing dam," Representative Adams said.

"Won't that increase the size of the lake?" a commissioner asked.

Adams said, "Yep, and that may solve another problem we have."

"What is that?"

Adams said, "There's a colored community that is breaking the law and is too big. They may be dangerous. Communities like this have started slave revolts."

The commissioners took a vote, and all but one of the nine members supported raising the dam.

The sleeping community did not hear the lake rise during the day or night. It crept around trees that would slowly drown. The six lakes merged into one. Small shallow pools of water formed in low-lying areas. Mosquitos would soon make themselves at home.

Early the next morning, Patrick pounded on Frederick's door.

When Frederick answered, Patrick said, "You gotta see this."

The two men walked a short distance to the new-forming lake.

Frederick said, "What the hell happened? I don't understand. We have had some spring showers, but where is all this water coming from?"

Patrick said, "I don't know, Frederick. Wesley and I did see some men building a wall. We were fishing in one of the lakes."

Frederick began to wonder and asked, "What were they doing?" squinting his eyes toward the far end of the lake. "I better take Wesley and see what's going on."

The three men and Martha gathered outside Frederick's cabin and urged their three horses to a trot. Martha was holding on to Wesley on a blanket as a saddle. The ten-mile ride took an hour, and the horses were glad to rest and graze when they got to the new wall. There was a crew working on the structure. The man in charge wouldn't talk to them. A black man in the crew kept working, but he did explain that the wall was a dam that would provide water for the canal. Then they turned their horses toward home.

Seeing their log house, Frederick ordered them to dismount, loosen the cinches, and walk their horses the last twenty minutes to the barn. He was trying to avoid telling Lucy what was happening. Patrick rode on to his own barn. They knew their horses were starting to cool down when they quit snorting and puffing, and a more rhythmic breathing started.

There were three stalls on the right side of the barn they had built soon after their cabin. The horses seemed to settle even more in the familiar surroundings. Martha and Wesley worked as a team, and while he removed the bridle and replaced it with a halter, she carefully lifted each hoof and removed any stones or sticks that were stuck. Despite aching thighs, Martha was glad they didn't have a saddle at this time as Wesley went to help her dad while she dried their horse with a towel.

"Now, you can rest and eat some oats," she said softly. She liked toweling off the horses and chatting with them. They knew some of her deepest secrets that she wouldn't share with anything on two legs.

Frederick said, "Take these saddle blankets to your mom so she can wash them."

"But she'll make me wash them," said Martha, not looking forward to filling a big tub and plunging the smelly towels in water up to her elbows.

Frederick said, "Maybe you would rather stay home next time?"

"OK," said Martha, knowing he would remember if she fussed any more.

They marched into their small house together, and Lucy asked, "Where have the three of you been? And why is the lake getting bigger?"

Everyone looked at Frederick who was stunned but had to answer Lucy.

Frederick said, "It seems they need more water for the canal. They are going to store it in the lake," explained her dad in a much calmer voice than he had used at the lake.

Lucy said sarcastically, "Well, they don't welcome us. Now, they're going to flood us out. What are you going to do about it?"

Patrick wanted to go back at night and reopen the spillway. Thinking they would end up in jail, Frederick said no to that plan.

He suggested they go to the courthouse to see what could be done.

The next day, Frederick, Patrick, and Martha set off for the courthouse. They took a wagon to get supplies from the general store after the court visit. Martha got to go by arguing that a young woman might help their cause.

After finding the "colored only" door at the rear of the courthouse, they stood in front of the only available clerk. The clerk behind the counter didn't look up from the newspaper he was reading, and so they waited. After what seemed like an hour, Martha said, "Mister, can you tell us who we can talk to about the dike at the lake?"

"There ain't no one your kind can talk to," said the man, still not looking up.

"Why is that?" asked her dad.

"You have no legal standing," answered the man.

"What's that mean?" asked Patrick.

"Colored don't have a say in court. You can't sue anybody or be a witness," he answered, looking over his glasses.

"Why?" asked Martha.

"'Cause, that's the law," answered the man, adding, "You should go on about your business."

"This *is* our business," said her dad.

"Don't make me call a guard," the clerk said while standing. Putting down his paper, he looked around for a guard.

With a nod of his head, Frederick signaled Martha and Patrick to leave. Patrick opened his fists.

The supply store had a similar sign about a back door for colored. Patrick had a growing resentment toward these signs and the people who put them prominently out front.

Upon entering the back of the store, Mister Fox, the store owner, said, "Good day, Mr. F. Who is this pretty little thing with you?"

Martha knew that her dad hated being called Mr. F. and could see him stiffen. Sometimes her mom called him "Mister," just to get his attention or to be sweet. She guessed that Mister Fox did it as condescension. He called all his white customers by their last names but not Frederick.

"This is my daughter, Martha, Mr. Fox. She's been here before," he said.

"Oh, that's right. What brings you to town today?" Mister Fox asked.

Frederick wanted to talk about the courthouse, but he hesitated.

"We just need some flour, salt, and sugar," he said.

"I can fix you right up," said Mister Fox.

He pointed to some bags in different stacks, and while her dad and Patrick pulled off the big bag of flour and small bags of salt and sugar, Mister Fox began writing a bill. He did all the lifting for his white customers but not for them.

Mister Fox announced, "I hope your crops come in before your account runs out."

Frederick said, "We've been keeping our own records. Our numbers show plenty of money left."

Martha knew that their account had lots of money because she was keeping the records each time. Dr. Patteson had opened an account for each family, and with Martha's help, most knew what they started with and where they stood. A couple of families had run out of money, according to Mister Fox, and he wanted to see their records. Martha took a couple of papers from her purse and looked at Frederick for a nod before putting them on the counter.

Mister Fox looked at the entries showing each item, what it cost, and then a balance in a separate column. He said, "I don't know if these are all correct."

Frederick said, "We show these records to Mister Barmash at the bank every time we come. He says they have been correct every time. He has even looked in our wagon to see what we bought."

"Oh, ah . . . Well, Mister Barmash is certainly good with numbers and an honest man. Can you leave these papers with me?" he asked.

Frederick, shaking his head, said, "Only if you write out a copy from these."

"Never mind, go on now. I've got other customers to help," said Mister Fox as he walked toward a white woman who had entered the store.

As his horse trotted away from the store, Patrick looked around to be sure no one was within earshot and then asked, "Frederick, don't you just want to shake people like that?"

"No, I don't focus on people like Mister Fox. We have freedom but not equality. Equality will be a struggle for a long time. We are free, and we can use the front door of our cabin. We come and go as we please, and we can eat what we want, when we want. The clothes we wear are our choice now, and we can work if we want and rest when we need to. We can protect each other from harm. Those white folks can't do anything about our freedom now," explained Frederick.

"Seems like I still have a lot of bosses I can't get away from," said Martha.

Frederick said with a smile and a hug, "You don't have a master, and when you come of age, you will be your only boss."

There will be statues of Bill Gates across the Third World. There's a reasonable shot that—because of his money—we will cure malaria.

Malcolm Gladwell

Spring, 1850, Indian Lake, Ohio

Chapter 21
Two Sides of the Same Coin

Martha had always loved the lakes near their small farm. The sun shimmering across the water looked like a million angels. The water smelled fresh, and you could cup your hands and drink your fill. She often giggled underwater in one of the lakes while watching bubbles rise to the bright surface. The pines and willows lining the banks were like graceful dancers being guided by the breeze. Water lilies congregated like a silent choir in one calm section of the lake.

The special trails that laced their way around the six lakes had been Indian hunting and fishing trails. At least, her dad owned a piece of trail that crossed their property that was still out of the rising water. She and Annise loved walking along the paths between several lakes and discovered many flowers and sometimes, arrowheads.

Today, she heard some strange noises ahead. It was as if something were tearing through the leaves on the trees. Then she saw Wesley throwing rocks at birds in the trees. *It's fortunate for him that his aim is not all that good*, thought Martha.

She picked up a small stone and hit him in the back of his head.

Turning and rubbing his head, he said, "Ow! Why did you do that? Help me get one of these birds."

Before he finished his statement, he was hit hard from the side as Martha tackled him. The two of them fell in the grass and rolled over.

"The birds are my friends," Martha said, getting up and finding a fallen branch. She began swinging it like a club.

"OK, OK," said Wesley, dropping a small stone he was still holding as he got to his feet.

Martha kept an eye on her brother as he walked briskly back down the trail toward their cabin. She was glad to have caught him before he caused any harm to the little creatures. What would make him want to kill a bird was beyond her comprehension. The birds were also part of why she and Annise had loved the lakes.

Now, because, as Martha saw it, Annise had been killed by the dam that created one big lake and many marshes that spring, the new lake would never be the same for her. Annise had come down with fever and chills, and there was nothing Martha's mom could do when people in the community got this sick. Several of their people had died, but Martha had hoped that Annise would get well.

The white doctor in town had refused to come because he said colored didn't get malaria like whites. Martha didn't understand why Annise had violent shaking and chills, and her body was hot to the touch. Annise had also been sweating a lot and soaking her clothes and sheets. The diarrhea was the worst part, and Annise's mom did her best to keep her clean and the air fresh. Martha felt like her emotions had been drained from her when Annise died. For several days, she no longer cared about anything.

Annise was Martha's best friend, and she looked up to her because she seemed so wise. Now that she was gone, Martha felt empty. She would no longer have her friend to explore the woods, and the two of them to find flowers together. They wouldn't row a boat together or even laugh at the stupid boys in the community. Her laughter at Martha's commentary would be missed the most. Their special places would not be the same, and Martha knew she would think of Annise everywhere she went around the lake. Thinking of the community without Annise didn't seem possible, and she had to remind herself that Annise was gone.

A service was held in the small church that they had built, and Martha had been almost afraid to go. Annise was buried in a cemetery where many of the freed people were laid to rest. Martha could not watch when her friend was put in the ground. Her family was relieved that her suffering was over, but they would miss her so much. She had been responsible for her two younger brothers and one younger sister, and that was a role that would be hard to fill.

As Martha was leaving the cemetery, Bil-Buck was waiting outside the gate with a casket. His eyes were red while tears rolled down his cheeks. Patrick and Pleasant dressed in black were waiting with Bil-Buck.

Now, the small lakes had disappeared. As Martha walked toward the new lake on a grey day with a chill in the air, the lake had become a dangerous place. The water was choppy this morning, and the leafless trees seemed like monsters waiting to grab her with their long talons. The water lilies reminded her of the flowers at Annise's funeral. She knew the small puddles were the worst places that bred the deadly mosquitoes.

Overcoming poverty is not a task of charity. It is an act of justice. Like slavery and apartheid, poverty is not natural. It is man-made and it can be overcome and eradicated by the actions of human beings. Sometimes it falls on a generation to be great. YOU can be that great generation. Let your greatness blossom.

Nelson Mandela

Summer, 1852, Indian Lake, Ohio

Chapter 22
Where Is Home?

A group gathered around yet another small grave. This type of gathering had become a frequent and unwanted occurrence. A third of the families and friends in the new community had died from malaria. The rising lake created perfect breeding grounds for the death-carrying mosquitoes. The doctors in town told them that colored didn't get the same diseases as whites, so, any medications they had wouldn't help.

"God is just, righteous, and loving. Please, God, look after the soul of this lost child," said Frederick at the funeral for Patrick's nephew.

Patrick wondered what kind of just, righteous, and loving God would snuff out a young child's life. He would have given his life in place of the four-year-old toddler. Sylla never told anyone who the father was. There were several candidates among the original men from the Warwick plantation. Whoever it was did not appear obvious at this time. Only one man had tears in his eyes. He was one who had been frequently hired out from the plantation.

Men had joined together to create this graveyard, and they hated all the graves they had to dig this spring. This toddler's grave had been particularly difficult for Patrick to help dig. Not because of the inevitable rocks, but because it was his nephew's final resting place.

That night, Patrick, Pleasant, and his sister were eating a chicken and vegetable casserole that Nicey dropped off. Sylla was not feeling hungry but managed a few bites with Pleasant's urging.

Pleasant was afraid that Patrick would get malaria. "So, what should we do now? Should we move or stay, and if we move, where will we go?" asked Pleasant.

"I don't know what to do. What do you think, Sylla?" asked Patrick.

"I haven't been able to think straight since my boy died," Sylla said, starting to cry again.

Patrick felt he might have to shoulder this decision. Sylla and Pleasant had taken over the household chores. Sylla had often used the excuse of looking after her boy to avoid doing anything around the cabin. Pleasant was proving to be a good cook.

The family had never made decisions before. They thought they were settled for the rest of their lives. Their log cabin on a small farm near the lake was to be their final home. Now, the deaths of twenty-five of the freed people from malaria and the likelihood of more deaths to come if they stayed had made this question a centerpiece at many tables. The community was breaking up fast, with families scattering all over Ohio. Their land, not underwater, was sold for five dollars an acre.

"California is a new free state," said Patrick.

"That would require another and even longer wagon train ride, and I'm too tired to be going on another wagon train. I barely survived the first one," said Sylla.

Patrick said, "The closest free state is Indiana, but they don't want us. That anticolored law passed, and we would not be able to get in."

Sylla mumbled, "I don't want to be too far from my little boy's grave."

Patrick didn't understand this attachment to a hole in the ground but said nothing.

Pleasant said, "I heard that Frederick's family is moving to Bellefontaine. Would you be able to work if we did that, Patrick?"

Patrick hesitated and responded, "I'm not sure. If many of us stay, it'll make jobs harder to find."

Sylla said, "Why don't you go to town and see what jobs there are."

Patrick was not optimistic about finding work. *My skills are from farming, but maybe some farmer needs help.* Pleasant and Sylla were hoping he would try as they looked at each other with their eyebrows raised.

Taking another bite of the delicious stew, he said, "I'll take our horse and ride up to town tomorrow. I can't promise anything. You two stay inside as much as possible. I don't want to lose any more family to those damn mosquitoes."

Pleasant hugged Patrick and whispered in his ear, "I'll help Sylla with the chores and cooking. I'll go wherever you want to live."

Patrick woke at his usual time as the sun came up the next morning and half-wished that his family was willing to move a little farther away, but he would go to town and see what was possible. As he rode across his farm and woods, he thought, *What a crime it is to make this land uninhabitable. I wish I knew who to shoot.*

Patrick's first stop was at a blacksmith's shop. He watched as the muscular man pounded on a glowing yellow-orange horseshoe. When the blacksmith dipped the shoe into a bucket of water that immediately boiled over, Patrick said, "I know a little about blacksmithing. Could you use some help?"

"I like my work because I work alone. Plan to keep it that way," the smithy said.

"I really need a job," Patrick said.

"Try the hotel on the Columbus road. They hire colored once in a while," suggested the smithy.

Patrick knew where the hotel was from previous visits to Bellefontaine because it was in the same block as the general store. The hotel had a sign out front that read "Colored enter in the rear." Patrick didn't bother getting off his horse but kept riding on Main Street.

After leaving the small shops and bank area, he saw a woman trying to open a gate to her walk. Patrick said, "Do you need some help?"

"Oh my, young man. If you can open this gate, I will be very grateful," the woman said.

Patrick dismounted and looped the reins over a fence rail. He walked up to the gate and saw that a hinge had come loose and was causing the gate to bind between the two fence posts. Picking up a water-polished stone and holding the gate up from the bottom, he tapped the nails back in place, and the gate easily swung open.

He said, "That will hold for a while, but you will need to put in longer nails and move the hinge up on the gate."

"If you would fix it better, I would be glad to pay you for your troubles," she said and added, "I'm Miss Dover."

"I'm Patrick Weaver, and I've been looking for work."

"Well, Mister Weaver, you have come to the right place. My husband died two years ago last week. This place has been falling apart, and I need someone to help with all kinds of chores. Do you know how to plant a vegetable garden?"

"I've been a farmer for several years," he answered.

"When can you start?" asked Miss Dover.

"I can work the rest of today. Then my family and I will need to move to town. I can come back to work the day after tomorrow," he said.

"Do you have a place?" Miss Dover asked.

"Not yet, but we'll find something," said Patrick.

Miss Dover said, "Don't move yet. Let's see how you work out, and I might be able to help."

Patrick worked for the rest of the week, and Miss Dover seemed pleased. She showed him a small cottage behind her barn that he could have in exchange for fixing it up. Patrick liked Miss Dover and liked having a job that would use his skills. The house behind the barn was a frame house with clapboard siding. It would need to be painted inside and out and probably need a new roof. He hoped the three of them could make it home.

Miss Dover showed him the little house. It smelled musty and had two bedrooms. She seemed apologetic about the outside privy. The kitchen was one wall in a modest living and dining room. Patrick guessed that their limited furniture would work.

"You will have to fix this up on your own time if you want to live in the house," said Miss Dover. "I want you to paint my house, and you can use extra paint for the cottage."

"My woman and my sister will enjoy fixing up a new home."

"Does either of them cook?"

"If you are looking for a cook, I can recommend my woman,

Pleasant, who's a good cook," said Patrick, remembering many meals Pleasant had prepared in their cabin.

After Patrick told Pleasant and Sylla about the small house, Sylla said, "I'm happy not to be moving far away." Pleasant was concerned that Miss Dover might not like her cooking.

PART IV

The War Years
Who won the battle at Jubal Early's redoubt?

Prejudice is a great time saver. You can form opinions without having to get the facts.

E. B. White

July 1862, Bellefontaine, Ohio

Chapter 23
Oh Yes, I Can

A few families moved to Bellefontaine ten years ago, but most left for other parts of Ohio. For eight years, Martha served as a teacher after her shift at the Thomas Hughes Hotel. The hotel work involved cleaning rooms, changing beds, laundry, and helping in the kitchen. She was usually done by two in the afternoon and could teach reading and math in the afternoons to students in grades three to six. The other teachers were always glad to see her.

The war had changed everything. There were no more traveling salesmen because they had gone to war, and almost no one was traveling. The hotel had told her she was not needed anymore, and they were closing. Although Martha was living with her parents, she was twenty-six years old and needed a job.

The shop Martha was looking for was on the edge of town in

a dilapidated shack. It was next to a blacksmith's shop. Martha was peering through the backdoor window of a rifle shop. She was watching Meshack Moxley, a free black, who lived in Bellefontaine. He was an important man because he made good rifles. Martha didn't want the rifle maker to know how desperate she was to earn some money and only looked in when he was busy with one of his rifles.

On her tiptoes, she took another peek, but this time no one was there.

"What are you doin' on my back stoop?" a voice demanded.

"Oh, just looking for the man who makes the rifles," Martha said.

"Well, you just found him. What you want?" the man asked.

He was a stocky man with big hands and muscular arms. He was sweating from his labors and was tapping his foot while waiting for a reply.

"I want a job. I could clean your shop, and I can help you make your famous rifles," Martha said firmly, with her hands on her hips.

He started laughing and almost couldn't talk. When he settled a little, he wheezed, "The shop needs cleanin'. You a girl and you don't know nuttin' about rifles," he said, trying to stop laughing.

"If I show you that I do know how to handle a rifle, will you give me a chance?" she said with both hands still on her hips.

"How you gonna show me?" he asked with a big grin. Then he added, "You sure are pretty enough, but you don't look like no gunslinger to me. You could almost pass for a whitey."

"So I've been told. How about we have a clean and load contest?" she offered.

"OK. Come on inside, but if you get hurt, it ain't my doin'," he said, walking rapidly to his front door.

As she entered the store for the first time, she could smell sawdust mixed with oil and something metallic.

"Pick a rifle you can lift and git some stuff to load with," said Moxley.

He didn't say what to use to load with. She scanned a shelf and found what would be necessary. The rifle she selected had its own rod to help cram wadding paper and the ball deep in the barrel. She grabbed a couple of percussion caps that she knew would work in his Springfield-style rifle. Martha was aware that another man was in the office but stayed focused on her task.

"I see you know how clean and load one," said Moxley, raising one eyebrow. He added, "Your daddy teach you?"

"No, my older brother," Martha said, finishing up. She knew that wasn't the whole story, but she doubted he would believe that as a slave, she had learned from her daddy in order to hunt rabbits and squirrels on the plantation.

"Yu'all one of them families what was flooded out, ain't you?" he asked.

She nodded. He had loaded a rifle from the same rack, but Martha was just as fast. Then he left the store, and Martha followed. They went around back, where he looked for a target. Not seeing anything that appealed to him, he took his hat and walked down the alley and placed it on a fence post.

"You go first," he said.

"I don't want to waste your fine hat," she said.

"Yu ain't gonna hit nuttin'," he said.

He nodded, and Martha, while holding the rifle, looked down the long barrel, and using the silver blade site, she aimed the rifle. She aimed slightly to the right to accommodate a breeze and directly at his hat about fifty yards away. She was glad he had not stepped off 300 yards because while the rifle could carry that distance, its accuracy would not be as good. She squeezed the trigger—*BLAM!*

The mini ball made a small hole in the center of the straw hat and blew the band and several pieces of straw off the hat as it exited the back.

"Ah, damn, you got a job, and I'm out a hat," he said, walking down the alley to retrieve the tattered hat.

"My first name is Meshack, but folks around here call me Mose. You can call me Mose," he said as they entered his workshop.

The man who was still in the shop said, "I'm William, his son. I saw the shot out back. It gave me a good laugh. I'm the one who saw you and told Dad someone was out there. By the way, that was *my* hat," he said, still laughing.

"Oh, I'm sorry. I can't afford to buy you a new one just yet," said Martha looking down.

"You can start tomorrow if you are available. How does eight in the morning sound?" said Mose.

"I'll be here. How did you get started in gun-making?" Martha asked.

"I make rifles here, not guns. I learned how to make them on a plantation in Virginia as a slave. When I ran away, a kind Quaker, Mr. Williams, who lived in Pickle Town, took me in and hid me in a secret room in his basement," Mose said casually.

"Dad, it's Pickrelltown," William said.

Martha was watching Mose and his grown son, who was bigger than he was, spar a little like her family members had done many times.

"I'll never learn how to say that. So, I told Mr. Williams and his wife I was concerned about my family. I felt the master would break up my family and sell them off. After what seemed like an eternity to me, he decided to find my family, and to my undying gratitude, he found them and bought them for me," Mose said, more earnestly.

"Dad made a rifle for them as a way of thanking them," said William proudly.

Mose asked, "Where you been working?"

"Tom Hughes's place."

"Cleaning that hotel is like what we need. Wear old clothes. We need someone to clean up this place, but not in a pretty dress," said Mose, turning to a workbench and starting to fit a barrel into a wood stock.

"Dad runs back and forth to Richmond Dale, so we get some rest around here," said William with a smile.

"Not today you won't," said Mose, pointing to a stock that Martha guessed needed some work.

Martha wanted to smile, not laugh, but she needed the work and bit her lip so hard that it began to bleed.

"Don't git no blood on that rifle," he said, seeing her lip. "I'll pay five dollars a month, and you can start tomorrow. There's a big demand for rifles, and you will need to be here ten or twelve hours a day. Can you do that?"

"Yes sir, Mister Moxley. May I have a small advance to buy some food for my family?"

Without saying a word, Mose reached in his pocket and handed her a dollar bill.

"Oh, thank you so much. This means a lot to me, and I'll be here early," said Martha, while almost bowing.

She picked up a loaf of bread, some potatoes, and a chicken on her way home.

The next morning Martha was given the job of cleaning the shop. She thought, *I'm going to have to sweep and dust this entire shop regularly. The first time around has required an extra effort.*

"When did you last sweep this shop?" Martha asked.

"I ain't had time to sweep," said Mose.

When she finished cleaning late in the afternoon, she was assigned to sand the curly maple stock. Martha chose to work outside on the back stoop to keep the dust down inside the shop. He peered out the back door. Martha smiled, and she saw a very slight smile on Mose's face. She was happy to have the work despite his gruffness. He was fair with her, and he chased away any boys that came by to flirt.

Slave marriages had neither legal standing nor protection from the abuses and restrictions imposed on them by slave owners. Slave husbands and wives, without legal recourse, could be separated or sold at their master's will. Couples who resided on different plantations were allowed to visit only with the consent of their owners.

Archives.gov

Spring 1863, Bellefontaine, Ohio

Chapter 24
The First Recognized Marriage

Martha sighed when she came into the classroom, one of only two in the school for fifty children. She remembered sneaking a visit to the six-room white school and was upset with how many classrooms it had. All the students had their own desks and books and only one grade in each room. Students had paper and pencils, and the teacher had blackboards across the front of the room. Martha wanted to protest to the school managers but knew it would be futile. They lived with the notion that the schools were separate but equal.

Today was different, though. She was erasing the single blackboard and sweeping the room when Bil-Buck came in to pick up his daughter, Shirley. After some awkward stammering, he asked Martha to go dancing at the colored bar on Friday night. She remembered his wife was one of the victims of malaria before the community broke up eight years ago.

Martha remembered telling her mother she thought Bil-Buck might be warming up to something. Her mother expressed her standard concern that Martha was not getting any younger, and at twenty-four, she was way past her prime.

They had been on yet another date to the colored bar. After several weeks of this, Martha thought Bil-Buck only cared about having someone to dance with at the bar. He told her how pretty she was and how proud he was to be seen with her. So maybe that's all he wanted. I guess no more kissing and petting tonight while saying good night. Bil-Buck was one of the nicest men she knew, but she was thinking she had better start looking around.

Looking worried before saying goodbye, Bil-Buck said, "Martha, there is something I want to ask you."

If he asks me to the bar again, I'll tell him I'm busy.

"Will you marry me?"

Nodding her head and throwing her arms around his neck and kissing him, she said, "Oh, Bil-Buck, I'd love to marry you."

Bil-Buck gratefully said, "Bless you, Martha. Your daddy told me that we could marry in an AME church, and the state would recognize our marriage."

Surprised, Martha said, "You talked to him before me?"

"I wanted to be sure he would say yes, but . . . ah . . . your yes matters most."

"You barely got out of that privy, boy."

Bil-Buck added, "Ohio allows marriages among colored. They will issue us a license with our names. We will be the first of all the families who were freed to be officially married."

Martha said, smiling, "Like manumission papers, except free to be lovers."

"Yea . . . a-and free to raise a family? I hope you want kids."

"Of course, I do. You know how much I like teaching kids."

"I adore that about you. Helping me learn to read is when I fell for you."

"You fell harder for someone else."

"Yea, she was very affectionate. When she became pregnant, I moved in with her. Her death was hard for me."

Not wanting to hear more, Martha said, "I bet everyone will come. Oh God, what will I wear?"

"I'm sure your momma will help. She invited me to dinner tomorrow tonight. Guessed you would say yes."

With her head on his chest, Martha said, "She knew too? New rule. From now on, I'm first to know."

After a passionate good night, Martha went into the living room where her smiling parents greeted her. "No surprise here," she said and turned to the important issue. "Mom, can you help me with a dress? Bil-Buck thought you might."

With a sheepish grin, Lucy said, "Give your daddy another hug, and I'll be right back."

She returned, beaming, holding a white gown. "We have been working on this for two months. There is more ribbon to sew on the skirt layers and the lace on the lower part of the sleeves. These four white panels ringing your dress are from the material the same as the shirts we wore as young slave girls. I guess Bil-Buck was impatient to be married."

Martha knew she was the impatient one, but let Lucy's hunch stand. Holding the dress up to see it in a mirror in their living room, she said, "How will I ever pay for this beautiful dress?"

"It's your wedding gift from the women and me," said Lucy.

"So, this is why you wanted to know how tall I was some time ago? Mom, are you and Dad going to get married?"

With a sigh, Lucy said, "We've been together so long, it don't matter no more. Besides, Master Warwick married us, with his reading the good book and us jumping the broom."

Frederick, putting his arm around Lucy, said, "Until distance do we part is what he said. Now, we share the same last name, and that's good enough for me. Most stores assume we are married. Most folks don't know that where we lived as slaves, they had laws against slaves getting married."

Martha said, "Bil-Buck said we'd be first in our community. Is that true?"

Beaming, Lucy said, "We don't hear from the other folks who moved away. But for the few families here, it's exciting."

The date was set for the last week in August. Bil-Buck and Martha were given a few days off by their bosses. The wedding was planned for their new AME church in Bellefontaine, and all the new neighbors and friends came. There were bunches of flowers in large vases on both sides of the altar. A broken broomstick was next to one of the vases.

Wesley played his banjo with its new set of wires. The women's choir sang some of Martha's favorite hymns, and her song that helped them walk with the wagons was sung while she walked down the aisle.

Reverend King had come and officiated. Frederick walked Martha down the aisle and gave her arm to Bil-Buck. "Take care of my girl," he whispered.

The minister gave a short sermon on the importance of marriage, and pointing to the broken broom, said they were breaking from slavery restrictions. When the minister said, "I now pronounce you man and wife," AMENs were shouted amid cheering and clapping. Martha and Bil-Buck heard the preacher say, "You may kiss the bride." They were wrapped in each other's arms in an extended kiss cheered on by the congregants. The minister handed Bil-Buck a signed certificate. "I will mail a copy of this to the state," he said with a wide grin.

Later, the reception was in the back of the church. Frederick took charge of releasing pews to congratulate the newlyweds while Martha and Bil-Buck greeted everyone. Patrick and Pleasant came through the line, and Patrick handed Bil-Buck an envelope. Bil-Buck thanked him, turned, and laid the envelope on a table heaped high with presents and envelopes. Patrick gave Martha a one-arm hug and said quietly, "I see you finally caught one."

Martha kissed him on the cheek and whispered, "Are you man enough to marry Pleasant?"

Patrick looked as if someone had hit him in the solar plexus. Pleasant asked, "What did you say to him?"

Martha said, smiling, "I hope he tells you."

As people finished the line, everyone was treated to dishes of chicken, ham, beans, and sliced apples on the front pews. The party continued in the church late into the night, even after the newlyweds had quietly left for Bil-Buck's room in the house he shared.

That on the first day of January, in the year of our Lord one thousand eight hundred and sixty-three, all persons held as slaves within any State or designated part of a State, the people whereof shall then be in rebellion against the United States, shall be then, thenceforward, and forever free; and the Executive Government of the United States, including the military and naval authority thereof, Patrick recognize and maintain the freedom of such persons, and will do no act or acts to repress such persons, or any of them, in any efforts they may make for their actual freedom.

Abraham Lincoln

July 1863, Bellefontaine, Ohio

Chapter 25
A Man before His Time

Colored men were converging on their new church on a hot summer night. The windows of the building were bright. Two blocks away, Patrick was heading to Frederick's house to take Wesley to the meeting. Patrick knocked hard on the wood door, and Lucy opened the door.

"We received this letter from Frederick Jr. today," said Lucy as she opened the door.

"No time for it now; we can't be late," said Patrick.

"Take it with you but be careful with it," Lucy said. "What are you thinking, Wes?"

"I don't know, Mom. I haven't decided yet," he said.

As they went through the open church doors, they were amazed at how many men had come for the meeting. There must have been twenty-five men in the room. Most had worked on their church for three months five summers ago. They were proud of what they had managed with little money and a lot of volunteer time. A few white families had helped by bringing some food on Saturday afternoons, and one man who owned a lumber mill had brought a couple of wagonloads of boards. It had a bell tower, but the members could not afford a bell. They would persist in saving money until one could be found. The church had two rows of pews and two sides and a center aisle. Each pew had square ends and hardwood slabs for sitting. There were similar boards that formed straight backs for each pew. Some of the pews in the back had not been finished and were just boards to sit on, held up by rough stumps. The poster said colored men between the ages of eighteen and thirty-five were eligible for enlistment.

There were some younger men they didn't recognize, but they knew most of the men. Bil-Buck was sitting in the back.

As they sat down about five rows back, a train rumbled past. Attempts at conversation were not possible. After the train had passed and over the growing din of the gathered crowd, Pastor Williams shouted, "Welcome. I'm finally glad to see some of you in church. If you can't hear in the back, feel free to move to some of these front pews." Several looked sheepish but chuckled at the pastor's chastising humor.

"We are fortunate to have a lawyer of great distinction with us tonight and two enlistment officers from the United States Colored Troops. Without further ado, let me present to you a man who understands you and has the ear of President Lincoln, Frederick Douglass Esquire," said Pastor Williams. Everyone applauded.

"Welcome, my fellow countrymen. Thank you, Reverend Williams, for your kind introduction. I must say there are times when I wish I could cut off Mr. Lincoln's ear to get his attention," said Douglass.

That brought even more laughter.

"I want to tell you a story before we focus on your questions. This is a story about a man ahead of his time. I'm referring to John Brown."

A murmur spread through the gathering.

"Yes yes yes. John Brown. Just four short years ago, Mister Brown invited me to join him and about two dozen other white and black men and women to help free our enslaved brothers. He had also invited Harriett Tubman, the great slave liberator of that time, to join him. However, she fell ill and could not attend the meeting. I thought his original plan of taking an armed force against selected plantations and gradually building an army of freedmen had some merit.

"Alas, when I got to the crowded, small farmhouse near Harper's Ferry, he unveiled a different plan. Now, Brown wanted to raid a United States military armory just four miles away across the river. No argument I could muster would change his mind from what I feared would be a suicide mission.

"I have some guilt for not joining him and making a stand. One thing I do know is that John Brown would have been the first soldier to enlist in the United States Colored Troops to help free your brothers and sisters still enslaved in the South."

"Amen amen amen," shouted the pastor, with many in the gathering joining on the third amen.

Douglass continued, "President Lincoln emancipated, that is, set free, some of our brothers and sisters from the chains of slavery on New Year's Day of this year. The border states like Kentucky and Maryland that were loyal to the Union were allowed to keep slaves while all the slaves in Rebel states were emancipated. Now, it is up to men like you to guarantee their freedom. Hundreds of emancipated men from the South had already enlisted in the United States Colored Troops when Union troops won victories in their towns. They have brought great honor to our kind and have contributed to the freedom of many of our people.

"This is your opportunity to right the wrongs forced upon us by that dreaded institution of slavery. As you may know, I escaped from the irons of slavery. For a variety of reasons, you are freedmen tonight, and one of the characteristics of freedmen is that they make their own decisions. This is one of the most important decisions you will make in your lifetime. Some of your families would disagree about what was the most important decision you have made, but they will gratefully spend the ten-dollar enlistment bonus and the regular pay you send home. Because our great Union has been at war for almost three years, many jobs no longer exist, and the USCT is a great opportunity for you."

Amid loud applause, Patrick stood up and waited with his hand in the air.

Douglass pointed at him, "Yes sir, do you have a question?"

Patrick asked, "I understand that we won't get the same pay as white soldiers. Is that true?"

"Unfortunately, that is true," said Douglass, amid a murmur that swept over the men. Douglass waited a minute and said loudly, "However, your Governor Todd is trying to get legislation that will allow Ohio to make up the difference to each of you. The State of

Massachusetts has already made up the difference for USCT regiments formed in that state."

Waving the letter, Wesley said, "My brother said the food was lousy. The uniforms didn't fit. Some rifles don't shoot straight. Duties given were all the dirty work. If Rebs catch us, we will be slaughtered or sold into slavery."

"War is not a picnic. If you are looking for a soft job, keep looking. We need every able-bodied man we can recruit to win the war against slavery. You join the fighting against the Rebs, and I will continue fighting for you in Washington," Douglass promised.

The men stood applauding and cheering.

"These two officers will meet with you individually here in the front and sign those who pass the physical to fight for our cause to end slavery," said Douglass.

"Patrick, I don't want to sign up now. Maybe later," Wesley said.

"Frederick Jr.'s letter is hard to ignore, but I respect your decision," said Patrick.

The majority of men were forming a line leading to a table in the front where the officers sat, and the slow process of examining each man began. To everyone's surprise, when a man signed a document, he was given his ten-dollar bonus on the spot. Most could hear the instructions about where and when to report for duty, that, in all cases, was tomorrow.

Bil-Buck left the church quietly as the line grew.

In the fitness examination, one officer checked his teeth. Another had each man walk a few steps and turn around. They were asked if they could read and write, and they seemed surprised when many said yes. They were tested by reading from an army manual handed to them.

"Do you have any questions?" asked an enlistment officer who was colored, after Patrick's equally minimal exam.

"Can I bring my own rifle?" asked Patrick.

"We have rifles for everyone, but if you have one you like, by all means, bring it," said the officer.

Patrick had bought one of the Moxley rifles that were known for their excellent barrels and sites.

The next man in line asked if he could bring his horse and was told that only the white officers were allowed to ride horses.

They wondered where they would be sent and what their chances of survival were.

Struggle is a never ending process. It is never really won, you earn it and win it for every generation.

Bernice King quoting her mother, Coretta Scott King

Summer, 1864, Shenandoah Valley, Virginia

Chapter 26

Is the Fight Over?

Two surgeons under General Hunter were watching the colored troops form several lines in preparation to attack a hastily made Rebel redoubt. If the Union soldiers could push the Rebs back, then their next stop would be Lynchburg. Patrick's duties were critical to the functioning of the surgery tent. When the surgeons saw Patrick in the front line, they knew he couldn't be stopped at this point in the formation. Patrick had indicated several times that he wanted to join the fight and not just attend to the duties they assigned him. He had been recruited because he could read, write, and because he was colored. White soldiers would not be asked to do his job.

Patrick's tasks in the surgery tent involved recording the name of a soldier and what limb they lost. Then he carried the severed body part to a shallow trench dug by colored soldiers. He also helped bring dead soldiers to a deeper trench and recorded their names. These bodies came from the recovery tent, where the men often died from infections and blood loss. Patrick had been told it wasn't necessary to record the names of dead colored soldiers, but he kept his secret list of them with the hope of notifying their relatives. The trenches for his colored comrades were not as deep, and they often shared graves with dead horses and the body parts of white soldiers.

The four lines of colored soldiers were ordered to attack. The military strategy was to have enough troops that didn't get shot to overrun the redoubt. The surgeons watched some men falling. One man broke rank and ran in a zigzag pattern toward the enemy. From this distance, they couldn't be sure it was Patrick. The head surgeon said, "If he doesn't get killed, I may do it myself. I need him in surgery. He'll be hard to replace."

A couple of the men also began running the same pattern as Patrick. Patrick picked a section of the wall where the Reb was reloading. He shot one as he climbed the steep bank. The second man to fall received Patrick's bayonet. Fortunately, his followers arrived shortly after Patrick at the top of the redoubt just in time to shoot a Reb aiming at Patrick. There were two bodies at Patrick's feet. The other Rebs saw their position had been breached, and they scattered toward a nearby woods. The final rows of colored troops arrived at the redoubt and cheered. The troops were ordered not to pursue the Rebs.

Patrick told his white commanding officer that he was required in surgery. With permission, he left the front line and headed back up the hill. He saw one soldier sitting up, holding his shoulder. Patrick put one arm under the soldier's good arm and pulled him to his feet. As they stumbled up the hill, the soldier shook his head, indicating he didn't want to go to surgery. However, he was no match for Patrick's strength, and as they approached the tent, the wounded man began to drag his feet. One of the other colored troops picked up his feet and helped Patrick get the man into the tent as he passed out. A surgeon took a quick look at him and decided his wounded shoulder didn't need immediate attention.

Patrick was ordered to begin his gruesome tasks for wounded soldiers now arriving at the tent in great numbers. He was often asked to hold the limb that was being severed from its owner. A soldier would grip his hand, which would suddenly go limp, and the arm would swing free. The men screamed in pain and often passed out, which was a blessing, but the surgery tent was never silent nor the ground dry.

Patrick dropped off the most recent basket of limbs and quickly returned to the operating tent. The surgeon's eyes were big, and his mouth was wide open. Several other aides and surgeons had crowded around a table where an unconscious colored soldier's jacket had been torn open in preparation for an examination. What they saw was a soldier who had wrapped his chest, but when the surgeon cut the wrapping, breasts bobbled free.

"Would you believe this?" asked the surgeon.

"It's a woman," said one of the aides.

The surgeon leaned over and yanked the soldier's hat off a shaved head, just starting to grow hair back.

"One other part needs to be examined," said the surgeon, unbuckling the soldier's belt and pulling down the trousers.

"My diagnosis is female," said the surgeon.

The dumbfounded men chuckled.

Patrick was as stunned as anyone in the tent but did not respond to the surgeon's joke. The soldier who had helped carry her said she was as brave as any man on the battlefield. In fact, she got shot covering for some of the soldiers. Patrick could see her wound was high on her shoulder and that she was regaining consciousness.

The male impersonator blinked her eyes and said, "I was afraid something like this might happen." She tried to cover herself and started crying.

The surgeon quickly wrapped her wound and covered her breasts with her jacket, then pulled up her trousers.

"You are lucky the bullet went all the way through," he said to her, then turning to the group, he shouted, "Get to your posts."

"Can I go back to my unit?" she asked.

"No, momma, you're going home! What were you thinking?" asked the surgeon.

"I joined because I didn't have a job. My husband is out here somewhere, and my family was starving. I knew it would be risky, but I'm big and strong and a pretty good shooter," she said.

"I want you out of that uniform as soon as we find you some appropriate clothes. You will be on the next wagon heading north," he said sternly. Turning to Patrick, he said, "Find a guard for this woman and have him find her a separate tent. Then get her some clothes."

Patrick thought this should be easy because the soldiers had been raiding houses and taking as much men's clothing as they could find. He recruited Norman, one of his tent mates, to guard the woman and told him to set up a tent just for her. Patrick started a request for women's clothing by asking some soldiers to spread the word that the surgeon had found a wounded woman and needed clothes for her. He returned to the surgery tent to find the woman resting in a chair just outside the surgery.

"How are you?" asked Patrick.

"It hurts like hell, but I'm more embarrassed than hurt. It was not pleasant to wake up in a room full of men staring at my naked body," she said.

"Follow me. A private tent has been set up for you," he said.

They slowly walked toward her tent, and Patrick said, "The man who brought you in said you were one of the bravest soldiers he had seen."

"I thought it was my job. Now I don't have a job, and nothing to live on," she said, with her head down.

"The army will get you out of here. I hope you can get home," he said.

Patrick told Norman not to let her leave the tent. In the morning, an empty supply wagon left the troops and headed north up the Shenandoah Valley with a colored woman in a dress, still wearing her army cap.

Most of the troops that had to be buried were colored. Their alive comrades would lead the next charge wherever the Rebs chose to fight. The speculation was that it would be Lynchburg. This town on the James River was a center for supplies and troops moving to various battles. It would be a major victory for Hunter's army if it could be taken.

The next camp was around the old deserted Friends meetinghouse in Lynchburg. The roof had partly collapsed, and it was not suitable for General Hunter, who had his command tent nearby. Scouts returned with news of a well-fortified redoubt with cannons and personnel about a mile away. They had been unable to determine the troop size. It was reported to General Hunter that several trainloads of Rebel troops arrived in much fanfare from the townsfolk. General Hunter had to consider his options, especially since his supplies had not arrived.

The surgery tents were on the far side of the crumbling church, downwind from Hunter's tent. Patrick thought he would not be needed for a while. He went to the church and found an officer examining piles of old records. He asked if there were any burial records and was pointed to a stack of records in a corner. The plan was to burn everything soon, he was advised, so he better hurry. The tattered books had dates on the front: 1852, 1851, 1850, 1849, 1847. Where was 1848 he wondered? 1846, 1845 . . . and then he found it . . . 1848. He opened the record that identified the person and the burial plot by row and number. Since John Warwick's grave was supposed to be unmarked, he wasn't sure John Warwick would be here. The space marked "no name" jumped out at him, and his exclamation got the attention of the officer. "Find what you were looking for? Hunter has issued a break camp order and a double-time retreat. You have to get out of here."

Patrick ran from the church to look for an unmarked grave that was probably John Warwick's. He could see the tents being folded. Patrick jumped the fence to the graveyard next to the meetinghouse and tried to get his bearings. Jogging down one row, he came upon a tombstone without any identification. Checking his notes, he guessed this was the grave he sought.

Kneeling, he said, "Master Warwick, I wish I had time to tell you all that has happened to us since you set us free. We survived the trip to Ohio. Dr. Patteson bought us land near a lake and supplies for a year. Then, after the lake was raised, we lost twenty-five of our people to malaria and many others who had joined us. We had a small community for a year, but now we are scattered. Frederick's family and mine moved to Bellefontaine, and Martha is finally married to Bil-Buck. I'm a soldier in a war with the South because I want to free more of my people. President Lincoln freed some, but they are only free after our army kills the masters or runs 'em off. I'm sorry I don't have time to share more. God bless you, John Warwick."

The Origin of This Book and What Is True

In 2010, a small group of people knocked on my daughter's post-Civil War farmhouse in Madison Heights, Virginia (near Lynchburg). They asked for help finding a slave graveyard. Based on the neighborhood's oral history, my daughter's family only had a general idea of where the graveyard was located. After cutting their way through the underbrush and struggling over rugged terrain, they found gravestones. The oral history also suggests that my daughter's farmhouse was built on the foundation of John Warwick's plantation house.

One of the people in the group was Kimeta Warwick Dover. She is a descendent of Frederick Warwick, a freed slave owned by John Warwick. Melissa Daniels, a white descendent of John Warwick's brother, was also in the group on my daughter's porch. Relatives of Kimeta's and Melissa's took DNA tests that indicated they were cousins. This means Kimeta and Melissa must also have a common ancestor who was possibly the Quaker, John Warwick.

Warwick's house was burned after the freed people left, and John Warwick was buried in an unmarked grave in Lynchburg but not at the South River Friends meetinghouse. The South River Friends meetinghouse has been restored and is open to the public. John Lynch was the founder of Lynchburg, and his grave is marked in the graveyard next to the meetinghouse. It closed in 1840 due to a split in the congregation regarding freeing slaves.

John Warwick kept families intact, as reflected in the probate of his will. Frederick Warwick was a favored slave, as reflected in the will.

The Price of Freedom was paid by seventy-five enslaved people who were given their freedom by John Warwick in 1848. As a Quaker, he felt morally obligated to give his slaves their independence upon his death and did so through his will. All of the resources of Warwick's plantation (one thousand three hundred acres, two mills, the main house, and a guest house) were used for the newly freed people. All of the freed people are named in the probate of the will, and many of their names show up in this account. I particularly liked Bil-Buck, Nicey, and Pleasant as character names. The main characters are their real names. None of the events in the book about them or the others are real, and any similarities are purely coincidental. Raising the lake was an actual event that affected the new community.

The will directed the executor not to leave the plantation until the crops had been harvested. Therefore, they probably left in the late fall. The freed people probably got to Ohio in wagons, most likely. Canal barges would not have taken them far enough, and the train rails along the route were of different gauges, requiring many changes. It is also likely that the blacks would not have been allowed to ride in the regular passenger cars, nor would boxcars have been desirable in the winter. The most likely means of transport would have been by wagons. Kimeta admits not listening to her grandmother's stories about the wagon train trip to Ohio.

In 1829, the Virginia legislature had authorized extending an east-west turnpike from Charleston to the mouth of the Ohio River. It already existed from Staunton to Charleston. Nicknamed the "central line," this turnpike was an essential east-west passage for people and goods until the Civil War and was the likely route of the freed people.

Under Virginia's manumission laws in 1848, the freed people had to be moved to a free state within a year. Transportation by wagon was probably arranged for the freed people from Madison Heights, Virginia, to Indian Lake, Ohio. Wagons would allow them to take supplies, tools, and household items. Kimeta has Haviland dishes that have been in the family since they left Virginia.

The scene when the parents have to leave a child to access a Quaker house on the Underground Railroad is based on the Linn

House in Bellefonte, Pennsylvania. Now the Bellefonte Art Museum. The girl with a broken arm would not have been able to crawl the long, low, attic access to the secret room on the third floor.

The executor of the will accompanied the freed people to Ohio. He purchased farmland for them in Goodland, Ohio, in John Warwick's name, and arranged provisions for a year.

The will preferred Indiana as a free state for the people. No one knows why they settled in Goodland, Ohio, near Indian Lake. In 1850, the Indiana state legislature passed an anti-immigration bill that would exclude any blacks from settling in the state. It is possible the freed people learned about this pending development and chose Ohio instead of Indiana.

At the time of their arrival, Ohio had a tax of five hundred dollars per colored person settling in Ohio. Providing farms and provisions for a year may have made it possible to avoid this tax. It was repealed in 1849.

Meshack Moxley did make rifles in Bellefontaine, and his work was in high demand during the Civil War. One of his rifles is on display at the Logan County History Center in Bellefontaine, Ohio.

A year after their farms were established, the Ohio Canal Commission decided to raise the level of Indian Lake to provide adequate water for the Dayton to Akron Canal. This decision caused the level of the lake to flood the lowlands near and on the Warwick settlement. The result was that one-third of the African American population died from malaria. If they had gone to court in 1850, they would have been told they had no standing in court. A newspaper article suggested raising the lake was done to destroy the colored settlement, but a few whites also owned farms that were flooded. At that time, there was a great deal of fear of blacks organizing a revolt. Today, Indian Lake covers most of the original Warwick settlement and is used for recreation.

Many freed slaves adopted the last name of their former owners.

Frederick apparently took John Warwick's last name for his family. Frederick Warwick's family was listed in the U.S. Census for 1850 in Goodland, Ohio, and he is listed as a mulatto. The family probably moved to Bellefontaine, Ohio, around 1851. Descendants of Frederick Warwick lived in Bellefontaine, Ohio, until Kimeta's family moved to Columbus, Ohio, around 1995. A family Bible with all of Kimeta's ancestors is in the National Museum of African American History and Culture.

Before learning about this story, I had been to Indian Lake several times to visit my brother who lived there. While boating on the lake I was unaware of what was below me, I crossed the area where the people's farms had been flooded. I have been back to the area since starting this book, and I have visited all of the Lynchburg sites described in this book.

The Civil War started within a decade of the arrival of the freed people, and many of them willingly enrolled in the Union army to provide opportunities for other enslaved people to become free. Patrick Weaver, one of the freed people, was recognized for his bravery in the Civil War. He never served with Major General Hunter as I had him assigned.

Hunter's Shenandoah campaign ended in Lynchburg when the Confederates fooled him into believing they had greater numbers than they actually had. This was done under Jubal Early's command when the same soldiers got on and off the same train several times. Each time a train unloaded troops, they got back on, and the train left and then returned. The locals greeted each arrival with much cheering and fanfare. Hunter, with no supplies and lacking useful information, retreated deep into the now West Virginia mountains to escape. Had he taken on the small Rebel army in Lynchburg, the war might have ended a year earlier.

They Fought Like Demons tells the stories of many women who joined both Confederate and Union armies. Their primary reasons were to follow a husband or to earn an income. As minority women, they had few options at home. This book inspired me to include discovering a woman on the front lines.

In 1976, my family took a wagon train trip on the Oregon Trail in Kansas. Our wagon master's name was Foard, and I did see him kill a rattlesnake with his whip while in the saddle. Foard also calmed a wild stallion so that it could be corralled. The much-younger ranch hands could not get near the manic wild beast.

Our wagons were the original prairie schooners, without springs, owned by people who settled in Kansas over one hundred years ago. A team of two mules pulled our wagon. We traveled a little slower than the typical wagon train in 1850, and I discovered quickly that it was more comfortable to walk than ride.

I started writing this book with the idea of using older quotes to start each chapter, naively thinking that prejudice was pretty much a thing of the past in this country. Then, a local politician in the US South called blacks, "Lazy people who want everything given to them." From there, public statements and actions only became worse up to the present day. Chapters now primarily begin with state laws, starting in 1604, that oppressed African Americans from the early 1600s until recently. Some contemporary quotes reflect the unfortunate status of racism in our society today.

Since the Civil War, blacks served in the Spanish-American War, World War I, and World War II, with no postwar benefits. Despite the Supreme Court, separate but equal schools continue today. Where blacks could live or not live was legal until 1966 and is more subtly continued today.

I'm struggling with labels for describing people. The human race lives on a continuum of skin color from light to dark. Using color for a race is misleading. The term "colored" is used throughout the book because it was in common use during the time of this book. "African American" suggests an origin that is not accurate any more than "Hispanic" is all-encompassing. I have taken two DNA tests. The one from National Geographic says my ancestors came from central Africa some time ago. Geneticists and anthropologists widely believe that we all did.

Text of the Will:

IN THE NAME OF GOD; AMEN:

I, JOHN WARWICK, of the County of Amherst being in feeble health, but of sound mind and disposing memory, do make, publish and declare this my last true will and Testament in manner and form following, hereby revoking and making null any and all wills by me heretofore made.

1st. The future condition of my Slaves has long been a subject of anxious concern with me, and it is my deliberate intention, wish and desire, that the whole of them be manumitted and set free as soon after my demise as the growing crops shall be saved, and the annual hires terminated—not later than the end of the year of my death—to be removed, or so many of them as I don't manumit and send to a Free State during my life, with the exception hereinafter named to, and settled in one or more of the Free States of this Union, under the care and direction my Executors hereinafter appointed. Indiana is my choice.

2nd. To carry out the above bequest—next after the payment of any debts I may owe, my funeral expenses, and the charges of administration of my estate, I hereby declare that it is my wish and intention that my Slaves shall, on being emancipated, have the whole of my estate now in being or hereafter to be acquired, whether real, personal, mixed or chooses in action, for the purpose of creating a suitable fund in the hand of my Executors for their comfortable clothing, outfit, traveling expenses and settlement in their new homes, with such provision for their comfort, sustenance and support afterwards, as the fund will provide, with the exceptions following, to wit:

3rd. I wish my faithful and confidential servant, Frederick, and his wife, Lucy, and her eight children; also, my cook, Nicey, and her three youngest children, as well as any others hereafter born in either family, to remain upon that part of the plantation now occupied by the said Frederick and his family, during the natural life of the said Frederick, should they not in the meantime elect to remove and become absolutely free; and I hereby set a part to their use in the hands of my Executors, the houses the said two families now occupy, and the other houses thereto appurtenant, with all that part of my land adjacent to the said houses known as the House Field, to the new fence near Samuel Turner's lines, and with the said fence dividing the said House Field from the remainder of my lands known as which lie East and South-east of it, to the Glade Road, and with the said road as it meanders to Lewis S. Campbell's lines, to and with said Campbell's lines embracing all the lands owned by me in the said boundary, supposed to contain two hundred acres—be the same more or less; together with necessary stock, provision and outfit, to cultivate the same under the kind management of my Executor, who, I trust, will treat these two families more as friends than as slaves.—Frederick being very infirm, and his family a helpless one, I expect the little farm and outfit will be a bare support for these families, and in addition thereto, I set apart in the hands of my Executors a monied fund of one thousand dollars to be put to interest upon mortgage security on lands or invested in State Stocks, the interest whereof, to constitute a fund for their better support during the life of Frederick; and after his death, (if they should not choose to remove before,) the said fund, with any unexpended profits, is to be applied to their ultimate removal and settlement in a Free State, which is in no event to be postponed longer than the death of Frederick, and the balance of the said fund not expended in their removal, is to be invested for their benefit in a joint settlement between the two families. I also desire my Executors to pay to Frederick annually out of the proceeds of the fund of one thousand dollars above described, the sum of thirty dollars during his life, not as a part of the support of himself and family, but as a reward for his faithful services to me.

4th. After the said boundary of land as described, set apart for the use of Frederick and family, and Nicey and her three children, shall no longer be necessary to be held for the use of said families, I desire my Executor to sell it either for cash or on reasonable time; and I hereby empower my Executors jointly, or either of them separately, to make such sale, to convey the land to the purchaser, and to receive the proceeds, which said proceeds will to the fund already created for the settlement of these two families in a Free State.

5th. I appoint Dr. Patteson of the County of Amherst, Dr. James T. Royad, Capt. Samuel McCorkle and Charles L Mosby, of the town of Lynchburg, Executors of this my last will and Testament, believing from their knowledge of my wishes and feelings, they will faithfully carry out my views as far as circumstances will allow; and having full confidence in them, I hereby desire that no security be required of them. Expecting Dr. Patteson mainly to carry out the true intent and meaning of my will, I hereby give to him the sum of two thousand dollars in lieu of the ordinary commissions, which sum, with actual necessary expenses, is to be regarded as charges of administration under the second clause of this my will.

6th. It is also my desire that my two old and faithful Slaves, Caleph and John, who, from age and infirmity, if they be unable to support themselves in a Free State, be permitted by my Executors, to reside upon the boundary of land before set apart for the use of Frederick and Nicey's families, during the natural life of Frederick and if after his death, either or both of them should survive, that my Executors allot a reasonable sum out of the proceeds of the sale of the said boundary of land, for their support, and that they give every personal and kind attention to them whilst they live.

In testimony whereof, I hereto set my hand affix my seal to this, my last will and Testament, this twenty-third day of February, in the year of our Lord one thousand eight hundred and forty-eight.

John Warwick (seal)

John Warwick died March 17, 1848

Obituary found in *The Hillsborough Recorder*, North Carolina, 1848.

Selected Sources

Patteson Family Papers, 1734–1906. Accession # 24295 and 41008 Personal Papers Collection, Box 2, Patteson Family Financial and Legal Papers 1779, 1784–1849, 1855, 1873. The Library of Virginia, Richmond, Virginia.

Papers of the Thornhill Family and of Thomas S. Bocock, Accession # 10612, Special Collections Dept., University of Virginia Library, Charlottesville, Virginia.

1782 Aug. 5; a deed between Daniel Warwick, John M. Warwick, Corbin Warwick, Frederick Warwick, James Warwick, and Thomas W. McCance on the first part, James Galt and Patrickiam Barksdale on the second part, and Julia A. Warwick and Joseph Trent Warwick on the third part. Text of the document found in Amherst County Courthouse, Amherst, Virginia.

Bibliography

Blanton, Deanne, and Lauren M. Cook. *They Fought Like Demons: Women Soldiers in the Civil War.* Vintage Books, a Division of Random House, New York, 2002.

Chevalier, Tracy. *The Last Runaway*. Penguin Group: New York, 2013.

Cook, Raymond. *A Journey along the Mormon Trail!* 2015.

Crocker III, H. W. *The Politically Incorrect Guide to the Civil War.* Washington, D.C.: Regency Publishing, 2008.

DeRamus, Betty. *Freedom by Any Means*. New York: Atria, 2010.

Douglass, Frederick. *Narrative of the Life of Frederick Douglass, An American Slave*. Boston: Published at the Anti-slavery Office, No. 25 Cornhill, 1845. (https://docsouth.unc.edu/neh/douglass/douglass.html)

Downs, Jim. *Sick from Freedom: African-American Illness and Suffering during the Civil War and Reconstruction*. Oxford: Oxford University Press, 2012.

Goodell, Patrickiam. *The American Slave Code in Theory and Practice:*

Its Distinctive Features Shown by Its Statutes, Judicial Decisions & Illustrative Facts 90 (1853).

Harris, Benjamin. *The New England Primer*. Boston, 1687.

Holmes, Kenneth. *Covered Wagon Women, Volume 1: Diaries and Letters from the Western Trails, 1840–1849*. Lincoln, University of Nebraska Press, 1983, Kindle edition.

Jacobs, Harriet. *Incidents in the Life of a Slave Girl.* New York: Barnes and Nobel Classics, 2005.

Jordan, Ryan P. *Slavery and the Meetinghouse: The Quakers and the Abolitionist Dilemma, 1820–1865.* Bloomington: Indiana University Press, 1998.

Miller,William Lee. *Arguing About Slavery: John Quincy Adams and the Great Battle in the United States Congress.* New York: Vintage Books, 1998.

McGuffey, William Holmes *McGuffey's Newly Revised Eclectic Primer.* Cincinnati: Truman and Smith (1836).

Northup, Solomon. *Twelve Years A Slave*. Lexington: Seven Treasures Publications, 2013.

Reed, Wanda. *Six Women West, Love and Danger on the Oregon Trail,* Sedona: Red Rock Publishing, Kindle edition.

Robinson, Jackie. *I Never Had It Made.* New York: Harper Collins, 1972.

Simms, Gilmore W. *The Sword and the Distaff: or Fair, Fat, and Forty.* Philadelphia: Lippincott, Grambo & Co, 1852, Kindle edition.

Smith, John David. *Lincoln and the U.S. Colored Troops*. Carbondale: Southern Illinois University Press, 2013.

Smith, Robert Lawrence. *A Quaker Book of Wisdom: Life Lessons in Simplicity, Service.* New York: Quill, 2002.

Siripun, *Swallow Barn.* Starry Night Publishing. 2008, Kindle edition.

Twain, Mark. *The Adventures of Huckleberry Finn.* Wisehouse Classics, 2015, Kindle Edition.

Webb, Harvey, and Willa Mae Fredericks. *Wash: George Washington Fredericks: Faith in Hard Times.* Sarasota, Fl.: TaHaHO Books, 2011

Whitehead, Colson. *The Underground Railroad.* New York: Anchor Books, 2016.

Websites Consulted

http://www.africa.upenn.edu/Cookbook/about_cb_wh.

http://amedja.tripod.com/legends.html

https://www.archives.gov/publications/prologue/2005/spring/freedman-marriage-recs.html

http://www.balchfriends.org/glimpse/JPetersIntroBkLaws.

http://www.brainyquote.com/quotes/quotes/g/georgewash146823.html?src=t_slaves

http://www.britannica.com/technology/prairie-schooner.

http://www.cbn.com/special/BlackHistory/Harry_Burleigh_Spirituals.aspx

http://www.civilwar.org/battlefields/batterywagner/battery-wagner-history-articles/fortwagnerpohanka.htm

http://www.civilwar.org/education/civil-war-casualties.

http://www.civilwar.org/education/history/warfare-and-logistics/logistics/pay.

http://cghs.dadeschools.net/slavery/anti-slavery_movement/quakers.htm

https://www.dailykos.com/story/2015/05/03/1381214/-The-most-racist-areas-in-the-United-States

http://www.eastoftheweb.com/short-stories/UBooks/LegSle. (Legend of Sleepy Hollow)

https://www.ebay.com/itm/1845-AN-ELEMENTARY-TREATISE-ON-ASTRONOMY-KEPLAR-UNIVERSE-HEAVENS-ILLUSTRATED-VG/192050845830?hash=item2cb71f5886:g:9SQAAOSw-0xYTbwR

https://docsouth.unc.edu/neh/douglass/douglass.

http://examiner.org/index.php?option=com_content&view=article&id=7972:historic-deed-leads-to-reunion-161-years-later&catid=34:local-news&Itemid=55

http://www.etymonline.com/cw/apologia

http://eh.net/encyclopedia/article/wahl.slavery.us

http://www.encyclopediavirginia.org/Lynchburg_During_the_Civil_War

http://www.freedomcenter.org/

http://hansenwheel.com/products/custom_wagons/CoveredWagons.html

https://www.hud.gov/program_offices/fair_housing_equal_opp/FHLaws

https://www.goodreads.com/quotes/tag/Patricks

http://historytech.com/project-portfolio/

historic-land-tract-mapping

http://www.history.com/topics/quakers

http://www.lynchburgonline.com/history.html

http://www.logancountymuseum.org/

https://www.cnn.com/2019/04/06/us/louisiana-black-church-fires/index.

http://www.miles-shute-kouns-families.com/histories/OHIO_RIVER_1800_1850.pdf

http://www.myersbriggs.org/my-mbti-personality-type/

http://www.notable-quotes.com/p/prejudice_quotes.html

http://www.pbs.org/wnet/slavery/experience/education/

http://www.indianlakeoh.com/Pages/default.

http://www.journalofthecivilwarera.com/papers.html

http://ir.library.oregonstate.edu/xmlui/bitstream/handle/1957/24654/ECNO1382.pdf?sequence=1

http://ead.lib.virginia.edu/vivaead/published/lva/vi00232.

http://www.lynchburghistoricalfoundation.org/index.php

http://www.measuringworth.com/slavery.

http://thinkprogress.org/home/2014/02/23/3321051/ole-miss-noose/

http://www.touring-ohio.com/history/ohio-underground-railroad.

http://trilogy.brynmawr.edu/speccoll/quakersandslavery/commentary/organizations/index.php

http://www.rootsweb.ancestry.com/~vaallegh/hist-cov.htm

http://rosemary-e-bachelor.suite101.com/quakers-and-the-underground-railroad-a91406

http://www.slaverysite.com/Body/maps.htm

http://www.soulcraft.co/essays/the_12_common_archetypes.html

http://www.spartacus.schoolnet.co.uk/USASafrica.htm

http://time.com/3707193/5-things-one-mom-wishes-shed-been-told-before-adopting-her-black-son/

http://ugrrquilt.hartcottagequilts.com/rr5.htm

http://www.us-census.org/image-index/va/amherst/1810/index.htm

http://www.washingtonpost.com/lifestyle/civil-war

http://www.wvencyclopedia.org/articles/225

Lightning Source UK Ltd.
Milton Keynes UK
UKHW021837200720
366872UK00009B/255/J

9 781977 227225